ORBITING

JUPITER

ORBITING JUPITER

GARY D. SCHMIDT

ANDERSEN PRESS

First published in 2015 in the United States of America
by Clarion Books, Houghton Mifflin Harcourt Publishing Company

British Library Cataloguing in Publication Data available.

ISBN 978 1 78344 394 9

Typeset by Palimpsest Book Production Ltd, Falkirk, Stirlingshire

Printed and bound in Great Britain by Clays Limited, St Ives plc

For Noah and Kathleen,
and for Carolyn

One

'BEFORE YOU AGREE to have Joseph come live with you,' Mrs Stroud said, 'there are one or two things you ought to understand.' She took out a State of Maine * Department of Health and Human Services folder and laid it on the kitchen table.

My mother looked at me for a long time. Then she looked at my father.

He put his hand on my back. 'Jack should know what

we're getting into, same as us,' he said. He looked down at me. 'Maybe you more than anyone.'

My mother nodded, and Mrs Stroud opened the folder.

This is what she told us.

Two months ago, when Joseph was at Adams Lake Juvenile, a kid gave him something bad in the boys' bathroom. He went into a stall and swallowed it.

After a long time, his teacher came looking for him.

When she found him, he screamed.

She said he'd better come out of that stall right now.

He screamed again.

She said he'd better come out of that stall right now unless he wanted more trouble.

So he did.

Then he tried to kill her.

They sent Joseph to Stone Mountain, even though he did what he did because the kid gave him something bad and he swallowed it. But that didn't matter. They sent him to Stone Mountain anyway.

He won't talk about what happened to him there. But since he left Stone Mountain, he won't wear anything orange.

He won't let anyone stand behind him.

He won't let anyone touch him.

He won't go into rooms that are too small.

And he won't eat canned peaches.

'He's not very big on meatloaf either,' said Mrs Stroud, and she closed the State of Maine * Department of Health and Human Services folder.

'He'll eat my mother's canned peaches,' I said.

Mrs Stroud smiled. 'We'll see,' she said. Then she put her hand on mine. 'Jack, your parents know this, and you should too. There's something else about Joseph.'

'What?' I said.

'He has a daughter.'

I felt my father's hand against my back.

'She's almost three months old, but he's never seen her. That's one of the biggest heartbreaks in this case.' Mrs Stroud handed the folder to my mother. 'Mrs Hurd,

3

I'll leave this with you. Read it, and then you can decide. Call me in a few days if . . .'

'We've talked this over,' said my mother. 'We already know.'

'Are you sure?'

My mother nodded.

'We're sure,' my father said.

Mrs Stroud looked at me. 'How about you, Jack?'

My father's hand still against my back.

'How soon can he come?' I said.

TWO days later, on Friday, Mrs Stroud brought Joseph home. He looked like a regular eighth-grade kid at Eastham Middle School. Black eyes, black hair almost over his eyes, a little less than middle for height, a little less than middle for weight, sort of middle for everything else.

He really could have been any other eighth-grade kid at Eastham Middle School. Except he had a daughter.

And he wouldn't look at you when he talked – if he talked.

He didn't say a thing when he got out of Mrs Stroud's car. He wouldn't let my mother hug him. He wouldn't shake my father's hand. And when I brought him up to our room, he threw his stuff on the top bunk and climbed up and still didn't say anything.

I got in the bunk below him and read some until my father called us for milking.

In the Big Barn, Joseph and I tore up three bales and filled the bins – I told him you have to fill the bin in the Small Barn for Quintus Sertorius first because he's an old horse and doesn't like to wait – and then we went back to the cows in the tie-up to milk. My father said Joseph could watch but after today he'd be helping. Joseph stood with his back against the wall. When the cows turned and looked at him, they didn't say a thing. Not even Dahlia. They kept pulling on the hay and chewing, like they do. That means they thought he was OK.

When my father got to Rosie, he asked Joseph if he'd like to try milking her.

Joseph shook his head.

'She's gentle. She'd let anyone milk her.'

Joseph didn't say anything.

Still, after my father was done and he'd taken a couple of full buckets out to the cooler, Joseph went up behind Rosie and reached out and rubbed the end of her back, right above her tail. He didn't know that Rosie loved anyone who rubbed her rump, so when she mooed and swayed her behind, Joseph took a couple of quick steps back.

I said, 'She's just telling you she's—'

'I don't care,' said Joseph, and he left the barn.

The next morning, though, when the three of us went out to the Big Barn to milk, Joseph went to Rosie first, and he reached out and rubbed her rump again. And Rosie told Joseph she loved him.

That was the first time I saw Joseph smile. Sort of.

Joseph had never touched a cow's rump before. Or

her teat even. Really. So he was terrible at milking. And even though I kept rubbing her rump while Joseph was being terrible at milking, Rosie got pretty frustrated, and finally she kicked over the pail because Joseph didn't have his leg out in front of hers. It didn't matter much because there was hardly any milk in it anyway.

Joseph stood up just when my father came in.

My father looked at the pail and the spilled milk.

Then at Joseph.

'I think there's something you need to finish there, Joseph,' he said.

'You need milk this bad, there's probably a store where you can get some like normal people,' he said.

It was the longest string of words he'd said.

'I don't need the milk,' said my father. He pointed at Rosie. 'But she needs you to milk her.'

'She doesn't need me to—'

'She needs you.' My father stacked his two pails to the side, then righted Joseph's pail underneath Rosie. 'Sit down on the stool,' he said. It took a few seconds, but Joseph came and sat down, and my father knelt beside him and reached beneath Rosie. 'I'll show you again. With your thumb and forefinger, you pinch off the top – like this, and then let your fingers strip the milk down – like this.' A squirt of milk against the metal side. Another. Another. Then my father stood.

A few seconds. More than a few.

Then Joseph reached under and tried.

Nothing.

'Thumb and forefinger tight, then run down your other fingers.'

Joseph tried again.

My father took over rubbing Rosie's rump.

She mooed once, and then the squirting began. It was slow and not all that steady, but Joseph was milking, and soon the sound in the pail wasn't the sound of milk on metal, but that foamy sound of milk in milk.

My father looked at me and smiled. Then he went around behind Joseph to pick up the pails he'd stacked.

And – *bang!* – Joseph leaped up as if something had

exploded beneath him. His pail got knocked over again and the stool and Rosie mooed her afraid moo and Joseph stood with his back against the barn wall with his hands up, and even though he usually didn't look at anyone he was looking at us and breathing fast and hard, like there wasn't enough air in the whole wide world to breathe.

My father looked at him, and I could see something in my father's eyes I'd never seen before. Sadness, I guess. 'I'm sorry, Joseph. I'll try to remember,' he said. He bent down and picked up his pails. 'I'll finish here. You boys better go back to the house and get washed up. Jack, tell Mom I'll be a few minutes.'

It was almost dawn when we went outside, Joseph and me. The peaks to the west were lit up and spilling some of the light down their sides and onto our fields, all harvested and turned and ready for the long winter. You could smell the cold air and the wood smoke. The pond had broken panes of ice on the edges, enough to annoy the geese, and from the Small Barn you could hear Quintus Sertorius at his grain, snorting in his bin. Rosie mooed inside the barn. Everywhere in the grey yard, colour was filling in – the red barns, the green shutters, the green trim on the house and the yellow trim on the chicken shed, the orange tabby clawing into the fence rail.

Joseph didn't stop to see anything. He missed it all. He went into the house, still breathing hard. The door slapped shut behind him.

Still, that afternoon he was back in the Big Barn. And he rubbed Rosie's rump. And she mooed. And then he milked her. All the way, even though it took a long time.

'Do you think Joseph will fit in?' my mother asked me later.

'Rosie loves him,' I said.

I didn't need to say anything more. You can tell all you need to know about someone from the way cows are around him.

On Monday, Joseph and I tried to ride the bus to school, which I'd done a million times and it wasn't

exactly a big deal. You wait in the cold and the dark, the
bus pulls up, most times Mr Haskell doesn't talk to you
or even look at you because it's cold and it's dark and
he didn't spend all his life wanting to be a bus driver,
you know, so you better shut up and go sit down. So you
shut up and go sit down and the bus bumps over to
Eastham Middle.

Like I said, not a big deal.

But that morning I got on and Joseph got on behind
me and Mr Haskell looked past me and said, 'You're that
kid that has a kid,' and Joseph stopped dead on the bus
steps. 'I couldn't believe it when Mr Canton told us. Aren't
you a little young?'

Joseph turned around and got off the bus.

'Hey, if you want to walk, it's no skin off my nose.
Two miles, that way. And— What do you think you're
doing?'

That last part was to me, because I got off the bus too.

'You're nuts,' said Mr Haskell.

I shrugged. Maybe we were.

'You know, I didn't mean anything. Just getting to know you, kid.'

Joseph stood still. His black eyes stared at Mr Haskell.

Mr Haskell's face got hard. 'Suit yourselves,' he said. 'It's twenty-one degrees out there.' He closed the door and shifted into gear. I saw the faces of Ernie Hupfer and John Wall and Danny Nations plugged into his ear buds all looking out the windows, staring at me like I was the biggest jerk in the world, walking to school in twenty-one degrees. And then the bus was nothing but rising exhaust down the road.

I blew my breath out, long and slow. I'm not sure it was even twenty-one degrees.

'Why'd you do that?' said Joseph.

'I don't know,' I said.

'You should have stayed on the bus.'

'Maybe.'

Joseph took off his backpack. It was pretty much empty, since he hadn't gotten any of his books yet. 'Give me some of your stuff,' he said.

I gave him *Physical Science Today!* and *Language Arts for the New Century*, which was sort of out of date because the new century was a dozen years old already. I pulled out my gym stuff, but he said I could carry my own stinking jock. And he took *Octavian Nothing* and looked at the first page and then looked at me, and I said, 'It's supposed to be hard,' and he shrugged and stuck it into his backpack.

Then he slung his backpack over his shoulder and nodded down the road and we set off, two miles, and it wasn't any twenty-one degrees.

Joseph walked a little behind me the whole way.

I won't even tell you what my fingers felt like by the time we turned at old First Congregational.

I looked behind me. Joseph's ears were about as red as ears can get before falling off and shattering on the road.

'Would you have known you're supposed to turn here?' I said.

He shrugged.

When we got to school, the late bell had rung and the halls were empty except for Mr Canton, who is the kind of vice principal who really wanted to be a sergeant in a foreign war zone, but he missed out so he's patrolling middle school halls instead.

'You miss the bus?' he said.

'Sort of,' I said.

'Sort of?' he said.

'We got off,' I said.

'Why did you get off?'

'Because the bus driver is a jerk,' said Joseph.

Mr Canton got bigger. Really. He stood taller and his shoulders spread and his arms widened away from his body.

'Mr Brook, right? Maybe one of your problems is a lack of respect.'

Joseph knelt and unzipped his backpack. He handed me my books. Except for *Octavian Nothing*.

'This means a tardy for both of you. You understand?'

'Yes, sir,' I said.

Mr Canton waited, but Joseph just zipped up his backpack and stood.

'Get to class, Jackson,' Mr Canton said. 'Joseph, you come with me and I'll go over your schedule. You do have a schedule, you know.'

Joseph didn't say anything. He followed Mr Canton, walking a little behind him.

At supper, I told my parents Joseph and I were walking to school from now on. Joseph kept eating. He didn't even look up.

'That right?' said my father. He looked at Joseph, who still didn't look up, and after a while my father said, 'You boys will need some warm gloves and hats. And probably some heavier sweaters. It's already pretty cold out. It looks like we're in for a wicked winter.'

My mother had them all ready for us the next morning.

Which was good, since this time it really wasn't even close to twenty-one degrees.

When the bus drove past, catching us a little after the turn by old First Congregational, Ernie Hupfer and

John Wall and Danny Nations with the wires to his ear buds flapping hard, pulled down their windows and they hollered out to tell us what idiots we were, and didn't we know it was like ten degrees?

When they were gone, Joseph said, 'Hey.' I looked behind me. He'd dropped his backpack and picked up a stone from the side of the road. He turned and lobbed it towards the bell tower of old First Congregational.

I'd never heard that bell ring before.

I dropped my backpack too. I missed with my first throw. It's hard to throw with your gloves on.

I missed with my second throw too. And my third. And, well . . .

'You're throwing off your front foot. Push off with your back.'

So I did, and the second time, I hit the bell pretty square. The second time!

'See?'

I nodded. I might have said something if my whole face hadn't been frozen.

And Joseph?

His second smile. Sort of.

After that, we walked to school together every day. At least, kind of together. He was always a little behind me. We followed the Alliance River – running dark and fast this time of year, and cold as all get-out. We'd stop at old First Congregational to clang the bell. If we'd taken a right turn past it, we'd go onto the bridge that humps over the river – or it used to. Now most of the wooden slats were broken through and a gate with a Bridge Out sign stopped traffic.

We turned left to head to school. And even though we didn't talk much, I think Joseph might have been glad I was there.

But I'm not sure all the teachers were glad Joseph was at Eastham Middle.

For Social Studies with Mr Oates and Language Arts with Mrs Halloway, he sat in the last seat in the second row next to me, since I sat in the last seat in the first row. Even though he was in the eighth grade and I was in sixth. He did go to eighth-grade pre-Algebra with Mr D'Ulney because he was great at math, but Mr Collum wouldn't let him into his eighth-grade science class, so we were lab partners in Principles of the Physical World. In PE with Coach Swieteck he lined up with the eighth-grade squad, which is across the gym from the sixth-grade and seventh-grade squads, and once he looked at me from the end of his line and shook his head because he hated being told what to do in PE, but he was trying. Fifth period, we had Office Duty with Mr Canton together.

At least in the classes he had with me, the teachers were careful around him. Not like they were afraid of him, exactly – they didn't hear what he said in his sleep at night, how he'd holler, 'Let go, you . . .' and then words I didn't even know. Or how he'd start to cry and then he'd only say a name, and he'd say it like it was someone he'd do anything, anything to find. Maybe if the teachers had heard Joseph late at night, they might have been a little afraid of him.

But they were still careful. I guess it was enough that once, Joseph tried to kill his teacher. That would make a teacher wish Joseph wasn't at Eastham Middle.

I'm really sure that's what Mrs Halloway thought whenever she looked at him.

Joseph had a picture he carried around. Sometimes he took it out from his wallet and looked at it. He held it so no one else could see it. Not even me. During Language Arts on the second day he was at school, Mrs Halloway told Joseph he wasn't paying attention, and she walked down to the end of the row and held out her hand and said he should give her whatever he was holding. Joseph didn't. He put the picture in his wallet and he put his wallet in his back pocket and then he stared down at his desk. Mrs Halloway didn't wait very long before she pulled her hand away. She closed her eyes halfway, walked back up to her desk, wrote something in her notebook, put the notebook in her top drawer, and then started in again on Robert Frost and stone walls and stuff.

She never turned her half-closed eyes towards the end of the second row again.

And there was Mr Canton.

A week after we got to school late, Mr Canton found me by my locker. I was trying to open it but my hands were so cold, my fingers weren't exactly doing what they needed to be doing. That's what happens when you take your gloves off so you can hit the bell of old First Congregational.

'Mr Haskell said you weren't on the bus again today,' said Mr Canton.

'I walked,' I said.

'With Joseph Brook?' said Mr Canton.

Nodded.

'What's the last number?' he said.

'Eight.'

Mr Canton twirled the combination to eight and opened my locker.

'Listen, Jackson,' he said. 'I respect your parents. I really do. They're trying to make a difference in the world, bringing kids like Joseph Brook into a normal family. But kids like Joseph Brook aren't always normal, see? They act the way they do because their brains work differently. They don't think like you and I think. So they can do things . . .'

'He's not like that,' I said.

'He isn't? Jackson, when's the last time you had a talk with a vice principal? When's the last time you got a tardy?'

I didn't say anything.

'Last Monday,' said Mr Canton. 'And who were you with?'

I didn't say anything again.

'Exactly,' said Mr Canton.

Mr Canton wore brown shoes that looked like someone shined them ten minutes ago. There wasn't a scuff on them. Not even at the toes. How would you do that, wear shoes without a mark on them?

'I'm telling you to be careful around Joseph Brook,' said Mr Canton. 'You don't know anything about him.'

He walked away with his unscuffed shoes.

'He's not like that,' I whispered.

That afternoon, I met Joseph at the end of the buses, where he waited for me. Mr Canton stood near the front doors, watching us. He nodded at me like we were sharing a secret.

Joseph walked home behind me, looking like he didn't want to share a secret with anybody.

So a little after we passed old First Congregational, I stopped and turned. 'You OK?' I said.

'What?' he said.

'You OK?'

'Why shouldn't I be?'

'Listen, what's your daughter's name?'

He looked at me. His black eyes. 'It's not any of your—'

'I'm just asking.'

He waited a long moment. And it sure was cold. Maybe fifteen degrees, maybe fourteen, maybe not even that. The bus drove by and John Wall pounded on the window to let me know what a jerk I was.

'Jupiter,' Joseph said.

I guess I looked sort of surprised.

'It was our favourite planet,' he said.

'*Our* favourite?'

Joseph nodded up the road.

'You mean, yours and . . .'

He nodded up the road again.

Joseph followed me the rest of the way home. My mother took him to counselling a little while later, and when they drove off, his eyes were closed.

SUPPER that night was warm and dark – sometimes my mother likes to eat with only the candles lit, so we sat in the flickering yellow. Later, though, outside, it was cold and bright. No moon, but the stars were so lit up, we didn't even need to turn the porch light on to stack splits for the kitchen wood stove. It only took a couple of trips for the three of us, and after we finished, I stopped in the yard and looked at the sky and said to my father, 'Do you know which one is Jupiter?'

'Jupiter?' he said. He looked at the stars. 'Jack, I have no idea.' He pointed. 'Maybe that big one?'

'Over there,' said Joseph.

He was pointing up above the mountains.

'How do you know?' said my father.

'I always know where Jupiter is,' he said.

My father looked at him. That same sad look in his eyes.

Joseph went inside.

If only Mr Canton had been there. If only he had. Then he would have known that Joseph wasn't like that.

Two

NOT ALL THE teachers believed Joseph shouldn't be at Eastham Middle School. Coach Swieteck thought he was terrific. When we got to the apparatus unit in the middle of November, Coach found out Joseph could do stuff better than any of the other eighth graders. Better than any eighth grader he had ever coached before.

Do a flip on the trampoline? Joseph could throw a double.

Do a handstand on the parallel bars? Not a problem.

And Joseph could balance on one hand for longer than you'd think.

Vault over the pommel horse? Easy. Joseph added a twist. Really. A twist.

Climb the rope to the ceiling in under sixty seconds? Joseph climbed it in thirty-eight, without using his legs. Which was the only thing Coach could show him how to do himself, because Coach had lost both his legs to a land mine in Vietnam a long time ago.

The first time they raced to the ceiling and back, Coach Swieteck won by four seconds.

The second time, Joseph beat him by three.

It was Joseph's third smile. Sort of.

'Don't crow,' said Coach. 'All you did was beat a legless old man by two seconds.'

'Three,' said Joseph, still smiling. Sort of.

'Three,' said Coach. Then he looked at the rest of the eighth graders, and all the seventh and sixth graders, too. 'And that legless old man can still beat the rest of you by a whole lot more than three seconds, so let's get to work.'

And just so you know, I could do the rope in under two minutes – which hardly any other sixth grader could do – and so what if I had to use my legs. You're allowed.

Mr D'ULNEY was also glad Joseph was at Eastham Middle.

Mr D'Ulney taught sixth-, seventh-, and eighth-grade math. He loved numbers and what they did and even how they looked, and sometimes he couldn't figure out why the rest of us didn't love them as much as he did. But I mean, who could love an equation – except for Mr D'Ulney?

On a day that Mr D'Ulney had bus monitor duty, I met Joseph at the end of the bus line and had to wait. Mr D'Ulney was asking Joseph questions.

Geometry questions.

Really. Geometry questions.

Joseph knew them all. I think. Or he could figure them out.

The next day, during fifth-period Office Duty, Mr D'Ulney saw Joseph and me sitting on the Office Duty bench, doing nothing – which is what most Office Duty periods were. So he scribbled a bunch of stuff on a pad and handed it to Joseph.

'Can you prove this theorem?' he said.

Joseph took the pad. He worked on it the whole period. When the bell rang, he took the pad to Mr D'Ulney's classroom.

After that, Mr D'Ulney brought a new theorem to fifth-period Office Duty every day. He would hand it to Joseph and Joseph would get to work.

Once Mr Canton saw Mr D'Ulney handing over the new theorem, and he said, 'These boys are on Office Duty.'

Mr D'Ulney turned to face him. 'Of course,' he said. 'It's so much more important for them to run around the school dropping off messages than be challenged to learn what great mathematicians have wrestled with for a thousand years.'

'You'd think they would have solved those problems by now,' said Mr Canton.

'It's not the solution, Mr Canton. It's the path to the solution that's fascinating,' said Mr D'Ulney.

He left and Mr Canton went into his office. He came out with fifteen slips of paper, folded over. 'You need to deliver these,' he said. 'When you get back, I want you to clean up the attendance files.'

After that day, we were pretty busy during fifth-period Office Duty.

So Joseph began to eat lunch in Mr D'Ulney's room.

Mr D'Ulney said that maybe, by the end of the school year, he'd throw a little calculus at him.

Those were the two teachers who liked Joseph.

JOSEPH never talked about his family, but I met his father. Joseph wasn't home because he was at counselling. We were getting ready to milk, and I was cleaning the stalls in the Big Barn when suddenly he was right next to me, standing by the manure traps. As soon as I saw him, I knew he was Joseph's father. Same black eyes.

'Joe around?' he said.

The cows looked over and their eyes got big and their tails swished and they started to hold their heads up and moo, which means they're pretty upset. Cows don't like strangers near the tie-up. They especially don't like strangers near the tie-up when they're about to be milked. Unless they're the right kind of strangers – like Joseph was.

'No,' I said.

'They got you doing chores, huh?' he said. 'What are you here for?'

Dahlia stamped her hind foot. When Dahlia stamps her hind foot, you know she's really upset.

'I live here,' I said.

'I figured you live here. I mean before.'

The milk pails clanged down behind me. It was my father. He was rubbing Dahlia's rump because she loves it almost as much as Rosie does. It always calms her right down.

'You Joseph's father?' he said.

'That's right.'

My father nodded. 'Jack,' he said, 'you come back over here and spread some more shavings for Rosie, would you?' Then he said to Joseph's father, 'You're not supposed to be here.'

'I came to see what kind of a hellhole they put my son into.'

'Like I said, you're not supposed to be here.'

'You have him shovelling manure, too? Is that what you get out of this? A bunch of kids who have to shovel manure for you?'

My father took his glasses off and rubbed his eyes. 'We're taking good care of Joseph,' he said, 'and now it's time for you to go.'

'You know, I can—'

'I'm sure you can, but like I said, now it's time for you to go.'

My father put his glasses back on and they looked at each other for a while. Then Joseph's father said a few words I'm not allowed to say, and he looked at me. When my father took a step towards him, he said a few more words I'm not allowed to say, and left.

Dahlia was watching the whole time. If Joseph's father had come within range, you know he'd have limped out of that barn.

Like I said, you can tell a whole lot about someone from the way cows are around him.

B Y the end of November, it looked like my father was right: we were in for a wicked winter. It snowed hard on Thanksgiving Day, maybe nine or ten inches, and then another couple of inches over the weekend. And it was cold. Fifteen on Thanksgiving Day, ten on the Saturday after, and then up to twelve on Sunday – 'a regular heat wave,' said my father.

When it's that cold, you're glad to lean in to your warm cow in the morning. And Joseph did – after rubbing Rosie's rump and listening to her say she loved him. He always milked her first now. Morning and afternoon. Sometimes I wondered if he was still so slow at it just because she loved him and told him so and Joseph didn't want to hurry any of that up.

Maybe.

It stayed cold that Monday, and even though it was pretty bright out, there were snowflakes in the air that afternoon again, drifting like they didn't care if they landed. The bus passed us at old First Congregational while we were heading home. Its windows were all fogged up, but I could hear Mr Haskell yelling at John Wall over the diesel to Close That Window, Close It Right Now – because John Wall had opened it to throw a snowball he'd smuggled aboard.

His throw, by the way, didn't even come close. Probably because he didn't throw off his back foot.

The bus rolled off through the high snow, and when it was gone, everything around us was only white. The ground, the trees, the clapboard of the church, the sky. Even the Alliance was frozen white, and maybe that's why Joseph dropped his backpack on the road, clambered into the high snow, and headed down to the river.

I followed him. If you don't know the river, it's easy to miss where the bank ends and the river begins. And the Alliance flows pretty fast, so it doesn't wear safe ice until winter has hung around for a while. And it gets deep quicker than any river has a right to.

I didn't think Joseph knew the river.

The snow was thick, but Joseph was breaking a path through it, so it slowed him down more than me. Even so, he stepped onto the ice before I reached the bank.

'Joseph, what are you doing?'

'Figure it out, Jackie.'

His other foot onto the ice.

I thumped through the snow alongside.

He shoved against his back foot and skidded along the ice, heading up the river.

Me following on the bank.

'You know,' I said, 'this is pretty new ice.'

He didn't answer. He shoved again, and then again,

and that second time, he didn't slide alongside the bank.
He slid out towards the middle of the river, where the
ice was darker.

'Joseph, I'm not kidding.'

It was like I wasn't even there.

The wind came up hard and Joseph unzipped his
coat and held it out like wings, but it didn't push him
along, so he shoved against his back foot again, and the
ice was slicker now, and he spun twice and shoved
again.

Towards the dark centre.

'Joseph!'

I think it must have sounded like I was crying. Or
screaming. Maybe I was doing both. But however it
sounded, Joseph looked at me.

Then he turned back towards the dark ice.

So I screamed the name I'd heard him say in the
dark of the night – the name I'd heard him say again and
again: 'Maddie! Maddie!'

He turned towards me.

And the way he looked at me – I don't ever want anyone to look at me like that again.

But he was so close to the dark ice.

'Maddie,' I said.

'Shut up,' he said. '*Shut up.*'

I stood on the bank of the Alliance, in all that white, and waited for Joseph to come. But he did not move. He did not move.

On the road above us, a car drove past. Another car, and then another – but this one stopped. A voice crying out: 'Hey, you idiot kids. What are you doing down there? Get off the ice!'

Joseph looked up at the driver, then started to jump up and down.

Hard.

Pounding at the ice.

The car drove away.

Joseph stopped jumping. Suddenly, he looked like he was all tired out.

'Joseph,' I said.

He looked at me again, and he started to come back, one tired step after another. He wasn't sliding at all.

Every step, the ice got whiter.

The winter I was six, I saw a yellow dog on thin ice on the Alliance. I was with my mother, and we were walking back from a breakfast potluck at First Congregational before it became old First Congregational. The yellow dog was out farther onto the ice than Joseph, but not much, and it had fallen through and its eyes were huge and it was grabbing on with its front paws, scratching, looking for something to hold on to. It wasn't making a sound. I told my mother we had to go get it, but she held my arm so I wouldn't go down to the river. Her other hand she held over her mouth. Once the dog almost got out, but the ice broke under it again and it was scratching like anything – until suddenly it stopped, put its head down on the ice, slid into the dark water, and was gone. Gone.

I live on a farm. I see animals die all the time.

Never like that.

I cried about that yellow dog every night for I don't know how long. I dreamed about that dog. I dreamed about me being that dog, and the cold water under the ice pulling my legs and dragging at me, and then my hands getting so cold they wouldn't work, and then the moment when I put my head down on the ice and slid into the dark water.

I always woke up then, sweating, wondering if I really had screamed or not.

That's why it felt like a nightmare when Joseph, maybe three steps away from the bank, fell through the ice of the Alliance River.

He didn't go under. He spread out his arms and caught himself, but the water splashed up around him and he went in almost to his shoulders and his eyes got huge – just like the yellow dog's – and you could almost see the current pulling his legs, and he started to reach for the shore, scratching at the ice, scratching at the ice.

I might have screamed.

I took off my backpack and dumped everything out into the snow.

Joseph still scratching.

I put one foot out onto the ice – he was only three steps away – and held on to the end of a strap and tossed the backpack out to him.

And felt my foot go through the ice and into the water and onto some rocks.

You can't believe how strong the current was under the ice, even just up to my knee.

I might have screamed again.

But Joseph had one end of the backpack.

'Hold it!' I hollered.

He tried to pull himself up onto the ice, but his left hand went through and he almost went under.

I leaned towards the bank, pulling on the backpack.

And felt my other foot slide down into the dark water and the current yanking at both knees.

I'm pretty sure I screamed then.

Joseph tried to push himself up on the other side,

and that ice held. I pulled again on the backpack and his chest came up onto the ice.

'Back up,' he hollered. 'Back up.'

But I couldn't back up. The water was rushing, and if I took my feet away from the rocks beneath them, I didn't know what would happen. Maybe I'd slide under – like the yellow dog.

Joseph's whole body was up on the ice now. He bellied up to the bank and rolled over onto the snow. He reached and grabbed my coat and he pulled, and I felt my feet leaving the rocks and for a second I might have screamed again, but then my back was up onto the bank and I was trying to kick – which isn't so easy when your legs have been in freezing water, you know – and then my heels were going into snow and not into water and I stopped screaming.

'Are you crazy?' I yelled.

Joseph stood and shook his whole body, like a dog spraying the water away. But he was still soaked. Already his hair was freezing into black strands.

'You are crazy!' I yelled again.

Joseph wiped the water from his face.

I stood too and picked up everything I had dumped out of my backpack – which was now as soaked as Joseph was – and already freezing too.

'This is how people die,' I said. 'They fall into the water and get dragged under the ice, or they make it out and freeze to death.'

'Then we better get back to your house, Jackie,' he said.

'It's Jack,' I said.

'Yeah,' said Joseph.

'Why did you—'

'We're out now,' he said, and started up towards the road.

But his lips were already turning kind of blue. And he walked like his jeans were frozen – which they probably were.

Mine were.

So maybe it wasn't such a bad thing that when we got to the top, Mr Canton was driving up.

He looked at us through his windshield like we really were the most complete jerks he had ever seen. He stopped the car and rolled down his window. 'Get in the back seat,' he said, and I got in and Joseph picked up his backpack and got in and he shut the door, and Mr Canton turned the heater to high. 'If someone hadn't called the school about two crazy kids out on the ice, I wouldn't have come here.' He turned around and looked at Joseph. 'It wasn't too hard to figure out who it would be, either.' Then he looked at me, and I guess you know what he was saying without him saying it. 'Take off your coats. And your sweaters, too,' he said.

Mr Canton drove us home. When we stopped, he told us he'd be talking to us about this during fifth-period Office Duty. 'Something for you to look forward to,' he said.

You can imagine what my mother did when we got inside.

'Stand in front of the wood stove,' she said.

'Everything that's wet, off,' she said.

'Quickly,' she said.

She ran upstairs and brought back the red woollen blankets from the hall cedar chest.

The scratchy ones.

'Underwear, too,' she said. 'It's not like there's anything I haven't seen.'

She handed us the blankets.

'Put these around you and stand there,' she said.

Joseph took the red woollen blanket and looked at it, then he wrapped it tightly around himself.

My mother fussed around the stove and poured two cups of hot chocolate.

'Drink this,' she said.

'Is there any coffee left over from—' said Joseph.

'You're too young,' she said.

Joseph drank the hot chocolate.

When my father got back, you can imagine what he did too.

Mostly at me.

'Jack, what do I tell you every winter?'

'Don't go out onto the ice until you say it's safe.'

'Did I say it was safe?'

'No, sir.'

'No, I didn't. Quiet, Joseph. I'll talk to you in a minute. Of all the brainless, fool things to do for a boy who has lived near a river all his life, this was the most brainless, the most fool thing you could come up with. If for one minute I could—'

'He came onto the ice for me,' said Joseph.

My father turned his face slowly towards Joseph. 'That's what we'll be talking about,' he said.

I don't need to tell you the rest. It had a lot to do with thinking through things and making smart decisions and not taking dumb risks for no reason at all and in fact not taking dumb risks period.

And I can't tell you what my father said to Joseph, since he sent me to the kitchen to get going on homework. But when they were done, Joseph came and sat down next to me. He opened *Physical Science Today!* and flipped through the pages.

'Sorry, Jackie,' he said.

That's all.

'Jack,' I said.

He took out his calculator and got to work.

THAT night, it was cold in our room and I was still sort of chilled. So I got into bed and under the covers about as quickly as a human being can do it. But when Joseph was ready, he stood by my bed, leaned his arms against the upper bunk, and looked down at me. Maybe it was because of the freezing water, but for the first time, I could see his scar clearly. The white line dragged down from under his right arm, then jagged along his whole side and into his sweatpants. I wondered if it went all the way down his leg.

'Jackie,' he said.

'Jack,' I said.

'Don't worry about Canton. Your father's going to call him. You'll be all right.'

'I wasn't worried.'

'I know.'

'I *wasn't*.'

'I know.'

My stomach unknotted a little bit – because I had been worried. A whole lot worried.

Joseph shifted onto his other foot. Probably the wood floor was pretty cold.

'And, Jackie,' he said, 'don't ever say Maddie again, OK? Her name is Madeleine. No one ever calls her Maddie except me.'

'OK.'

'So don't say it again.'

'OK,' I said.

'OK.'

He went across to the desk and turned the light off. It was freezing, but he stood at the window, looking up at the night sky, his hand up against the cold pane. Then, finally, he came over and climbed up onto his bunk. He lay without moving. For a long while.

'Joseph,' I said.

After a while . . .

'Yeah.'

'Why did you go out on the ice?'

After another while . . .

'Maddie liked to skate,' he said.

Then we both lay without moving.

Three

THE NEXT MORNING, my father told us that from now until spring, we were going to be taking the bus to school – no arguments. Since it was cold enough to freeze most parts of your body, I wasn't too unhappy.

To be sure we took the bus to school, he waited at the end of the road with us.

When Mr Haskell stopped and opened the door, he was grinning this stupid grin. 'Looks like you two got your minds changed for you,' he said.

Joseph got on the bus. He walked all the way down the aisle and sat in the last seat.

Mr Haskell watched him in his mirror the whole time. Then he turned back to us. 'I hear your boy had some trouble yesterday,' said Mr Haskell.

'Is that what you hear?' said my father.

'That's what I hear. I guess you took him out to the woodshed, if you know what I mean.'

'Actually, I'm pretty proud of what he did.'

'Almost drowning?'

'I guess you didn't hear everything, Haskell.'

My father turned and walked back up to the house. He didn't look at me.

He didn't need to.

'Are you getting on or not?' said Mr Haskell.

I got on, and the bus lurched ahead.

In the back, Joseph sat with *Octavian Nothing* propped up against the seat ahead of him. The way he looked, no one was going to be sharing his seat.

Not even me – because halfway back John Wall

pushed me across onto Danny Nations and Ernie Hupfer, and so I got up and jumped onto John Wall, and Danny Nations took off his ear buds and got up to jump on top of both of us. Then Mr Haskell hollered about how we could all walk the rest of the way and it wouldn't be any skin off his nose, and then he said something you probably wouldn't hear in new First Congregational, and we all sat down.

'You really fall into the Alliance?' said John Wall.

'Not exactly,' I said.

'How can you not exactly fall into a river?'

'I went in partway.'

'Jesus,' said Danny. 'That's how people die, you know.'

'Just up to my waist.'

'Up to your waist,' said John.

'Partway,' I said.

'You're nuts,' said Ernie. 'You are freaking freaking nuts.'

'If he's got any left,' said Danny. 'That's what freezes first.'

You can guess what I did to him then.

Another holler from Mr Haskell.

'I hear they turn black and fall off,' Danny whispered.

'Cut it out, Danny,' said John Wall. 'Jack's not the one who's nuts.' He nodded his head to the back of the bus.

'Shut up,' I said.

'You shut up. Everyone knows he's psycho. He probably dragged you into the river, right?'

'No.'

'What are you doing hanging around him?'

'We live in the same house, John.'

'That doesn't mean anything,' said Danny. 'He's going to be gone as soon as they find a place for him in psycho school.'

'Shut up,' I said.

'Maybe this is news to you, Jack-boy, but your foster brother almost killed a teacher.'

'Really, Danny-boy? Thanks for telling me that.'

'Every girl in school's afraid of him,' said John.

'No, they're not.'

John and Ernie and Danny nodded. 'Yes, they are,' said John.

'That's crazy.'

'What's crazy is what will happen if some of the eighth-grade guys ever find your psycho foster brother by himself. And you know which eighth-grade guys I mean. That's what's crazy.'

I looked at him.

'Don't you know?' said Danny.

'Know what?'

'You don't know what he did to Jay Perkins?'

'What?'

'They were in D'Ulney's class. Jay said something to Psycho about his girl, and in like two seconds he had his hands around Jay's throat.'

'That's not true,' I said.

'Ask him,' said Danny.

'I'm not going to ask him that.'

Danny shrugged. 'All I know is that Jay Perkins would

be dead right now if it wasn't for D'Ulney. And since D'Ulney blamed Jay for saying what he did, nothing happened. But that doesn't make any difference.'

'What is that supposed to mean?' I said.

'It means Jay Perkins is telling everyone how he's going to bust your foster brother up.'

John nodded. 'Psycho school better start looking pretty good,' he said.

You know what they say in books about your heart stopping?

It's true. It can. It does.

Danny put his ear buds back in as the bus leaned over to the right when we turned by old First Congregational.

I stood and went to the back of the bus. Joseph looked up from *Octavian Nothing* when I got there.

'Move over,' I said.

He looked at me a long time. Then he slid over.

That's how we rode the bus the rest of the way.

● ● ●

M R D'ULNEY was waiting when Joseph and I got off Mr Haskell's bus. He nodded to me and reached out to take Joseph's arm.

Joseph took two quick steps back.

'It's OK,' said Mr D'Ulney. 'It's OK.'

Joseph waited.

'Let's talk before the bell rings.'

They went together – Joseph walking behind Mr D'Ulney.

I don't know what they talked about.

But before PE class, Coach Swieteck gave Joseph heck.

'What did you think you were doing?' he said. Hollered, really. But you can hear everything in a gym anyway, you know.

Joseph only shrugged.

'You ever do something like that again, I am personally going to kick you around the perimeter of this gym.'

Joseph looked at him.

'How?' he said.

'You would be surprised,' Coach Swieteck said. 'Go get changed.' He twirled his wheelchair around. 'Mr Porter, Mr Boss, since you seem to have time enough on your hands, come over here and drag the mats around the trampoline. Mr Perkins, you set the mats around the parallel bars.'

Joseph walked past them, into the locker room.

'*Now*,' said Coach Swieteck.

The way he said 'Now' – it was sort of spooky. Like he meant something I couldn't figure out.

During that whole PE period, when I wasn't doing a relay up and down the rope – which, by the way, is a stupid relay – I watched those three guys watch Joseph. And they weren't watching him because he was so good at doing dismounts from the parallel bars.

Joseph looked like he didn't even notice, except once when Jay Perkins crossed in front of him when he was running towards the horse. Joseph twisted around so he wouldn't hit him, but he had to go back to do the run again.

I didn't hear what Jay Perkins said to him. Joseph didn't say anything, even though Nick Porter and Brian Boss both laughed like it was so funny.

Sometimes, Coach Swieteck was watching those three guys too. Sometimes, he'd make sure they weren't on the same apparatus that Joseph was on. And when the period was over, they were the ones who had to stay in the gym to roll up the mats and put them away while everyone else changed.

Later, when I was leaving the locker room, I passed Jay Perkins, who looked at me and knew who I was. He couldn't show it because I was just a sixth grader and he was an eighth grader, but he knew, all right. He gave me a long look.

I kept going.

At fifth-period Office Duty, Mr Canton had us both sitting on the bench outside his office, ready to fly with any incredibly important messages he had. But he didn't have any. And we had already cleaned up the attendance files. So there was nothing to do except sit on the bench while Mr Canton walked in and out and in and out of his office, busy as all get-out.

After almost a whole period of nothing to do, Joseph pulled *Octavian Nothing* out of his backpack.

He was reading it when Mrs Halloway walked in.

She looked at him holding *Octavian Nothing*. Then Mr Canton walked by. He told Joseph to put the book away. He wasn't here to read or play games, you know. He was here to work. And you never knew when there might be an important errand to run.

'I guess,' said Joseph.

'You guess?' said Mr Canton.

Joseph put *Octavian Nothing* back in his backpack.

Mrs Halloway watched.

'Being responsible,' Mr Canton said, 'means being ready to do what you're supposed to be doing, even if no one is watching or making you do it. Do you boys understand that?'

I nodded. I was supposed to.

Joseph was supposed to nod too. He didn't.

'Do you understand that, Mr Brook?'

Joseph stood. 'I have to get to class,' he said.

Mr Canton reached for him.

Joseph dropped his pack and immediately his back was against the wall and his hands up.

The way he was breathing . . .

'Don't touch him,' I whispered. 'Please, please don't touch him.'

Mr Canton looked at me, then back at Joseph.

'So you better get to class,' he said.

I picked up Joseph's backpack and handed it to him. His eyes never left Mr Canton, but he took the backpack and he followed me out of the office – a half step behind.

I could hear his breathing.

'Joseph.'

We both turned. It was Mrs Halloway.

'Joseph,' she said, 'we began poorly. Shall we try again?'

Joseph watched her.

'I'd like to know what you think of *The Astonishing Life of Octavian Nothing*.'

Joseph hefted his backpack up over his shoulder. Then he looked at me. 'I'll see you later,' he said, and he followed Mrs Halloway towards her room.

I didn't see him again that day until after school, when I found him at the back of the bus, where it was super hot and the windows all fogged. He had propped up *Octavian Nothing*, and he only stopped reading when we drove past old First Congregational. Then he rubbed the fog off the windows and watched the snow pelt the church and gather beneath the hems of its white skirts. He turned around to see it out the back window.

'What?' I said.

He looked at me.

'Just thinking about what it would have been like,' he said.

I looked behind us at the church.

'What?'

'Nothing,' he said. Then back to *Octavian Nothing*.

* * *

I T was still snowing and blowing when we went out to milk that afternoon, so Joseph rubbed Rosie's rump for a while to calm her down – plus she kind of expected it now – and she mooed to tell Joseph she loved him and then he got down to the milking. I did Dahlia. Most of the time Joseph milked with his eyes closed and the side of his face against Rosie, like she was a pillow. But today, he looked at me.

'So when are you going to tell me?' he said.

'Tell you what?'

'Whatever it is you're worried about.'

'I'm not worried.'

'And that's why Dahlia keeps stamping her foot, because you're not worried?'

'She's not stamping her foot.'

And of course, right then, Dahlia stamped her foot. Twice.

'She's just in a bad mood,' I said.

Joseph didn't say anything.

'Joseph, you know Nick Porter?'

'I know who he is.'

'Brian Boss?'

He nodded.

'Jay Perkins?'

Nodded again.

'Stay away from them.'

'Why? You sweet on Nick Porter?'

'Shut up. Just stay away from them.'

'No reason not to.'

Dahlia stamped her foot again. Twice, again.

'Listen, Jackie, don't worry. I've met all these guys before.'

'No, you haven't.'

'Yes, I have.'

'Where?'

'Stone Mountain.'

I looked over at him.

'They've never been in Stone Mountain.'

'Neither have you. Listen, with guys like this, you

take the first punch and break the closest guy's nose. Then the other guys get all nervous because there's blood and this is a lot more than they thought they were getting into, so they back off.'

'And if they don't back off?'

'Then they'd better be wearing a cup. Is that what you wanted to tell me?'

I nodded.

'No, it wasn't,' he said.

He waited for me. Kind of a long time.

'I'm glad you're here,' I finally said.

Joseph stopped milking. A minute later he started again – and the splash of milk was the only thing we heard in the barn.

THE snow stopped, but the temperature really dropped the next few days, so that getting up to zero seemed kind of hopeless. During the day, the air glistened with hovering ice. At night, the stars were razor sharp.

At dawn, the sunlight went straight up in a hazy column. And sunset closed the day with a quick wink. No kidding. One minute it was bright daylight, and then you turned your back and it was full dark, like it was trying to catch you.

It was so cold that even Joseph – who said he wasn't going to wear anything like that when he first saw the long underwear my mother had gotten him – put it on as soon as we got home.

Out in the Big Barn, the cows moved closer together in the tie-up to stay warm, and in the Small Barn, Joseph and I spread a heavy wool blanket over Quintus Sertorius, who shivered his withers at first, then tossed his head and nickered and stamped his front foot. It wasn't like Dahlia stamping her foot. When Quintus Sertorius stamped his foot, the barn shook and it meant he was happy.

When Joseph saw that, he smiled. Sort of. Number four.

On the Friday after it got so cold, my father and I

finished the milking while Joseph was at counselling, and then my father said, 'Jack, go get a couple of snow shovels,' and we went down to the pond and began to clear the ice. The snow was powder, it was so cold, and if there had been any kind of wind, it would have blown off like dust. It wasn't a big pond and it didn't take us long to clear it all, and after we shovelled, the ice beneath was smooth and slippery and light green and white. Around the edges of the pond, before it whitened up, you could lie down on the clear ice and see pebbles and drowned sticks and sand. The ice was probably eight, nine inches thick, my father said. 'If it were olden times, we might think about cutting it up for iceboxes soon.'

Then he shovelled away some of the snow near the pond's shore while I went up to the Big Barn and brought down three loads of wood. We got the fire started and then went to find enough skates.

We came out of the house with them just as my mother was driving up with Joseph.

'What fool thing are you up to?' said my mother.

'Come and see,' my father said. 'You too, Joseph.' He handed him a pair of skates.

The day was already hinting it would be turning off the lights soon, and the fire was reflecting across the smooth ice. My mother fussed a little about getting things started for supper. Then about how the boys needed to get going on homework. Then about ... But my father stopped her and she laughed and we took turns sitting on the woodpile and lacing up the skates.

Already we could see the moon.

It was the first time this winter, but it comes back right away. That first push and the feel of the skates roughing and sliding over the ice, the way your knees know what to do, the way you lean for the curves – it really wasn't a big pond – and the way you can flick around and suddenly your heels are leading and they vibrate with the ice, the heat on your toes, the cold on your eyes and the cold in your mouth, the shine of the moonlight and the firelight on the ice, and my mother and father holding hands and skating together side by side, and the first hoot of the annoyed owl, and a train whistle from far away. It was all the same.

Joseph was kind of stiff-legged at first, and he held his hands out in front of him for balance, but you could tell he'd done it before. He leaned into the curves like he loved the raspy sound the blades made. Once he tried to turn backwards and he fell on his butt. Second time, too. And the third time. So after that he skated around and around, even after my parents were off the ice and sitting on the woodpile, feeding the fire. Around and around, even after I was off the ice, warming my hands. And now his hands were at his sides, and around and around, and now his eyes were closed, and around and around, and we watched Joseph lean and skate, lean and skate.

Around and around, and I wondered if he was skating in the silver moonlight with Maddie. Around and around, and I didn't want him to stop, no matter how cold it got, or late. Around and around, and the sharp stars watched. And the low moon. And Jupiter over the mountains.

Until he slid into the bank by the three of us and the

firelight lit him and his face was so tight and my mother said what mothers are supposed to say: 'You're a beautiful skater, Joseph.' My father stood and kicked the flaming sticks together, and threw another couple of splits on, and Joseph looked at me and then at my parents and he said, 'I have to see Jupiter. Will you help me?' My parents looked at him, and my mother stood and she said, 'Joseph, you—' and he said, 'I have to see her,' and my father said, 'You know we—' and then under the sharp stars and the silver moon and glowing Jupiter, Joseph told us everything.

Everything.

Four

THIS IS WHAT he told us.

Madeleine Joyce was thirteen years old when she met Joseph Brook. She lived in a house that had pillars in the front and a wing on each side and statues on the lawn. Her father and her mother were both lawyers, so she spent a lot of time by herself in that big house when she wasn't away at her prep school. Sometimes she had a nanny who lived in the north guesthouse, sometimes not.

The nanny was there the hot summer morning the plumber came to change the showerheads and taps in the upstairs bathrooms. All five of the upstairs bathrooms.

He brought his son to carry the tools.

His son's name was Joseph. He was thirteen years old too.

Two days later, Joseph knocked on Madeleine's door. He had walked seven miles to get there. They spent the day together. They watched a few movies. She showed him how to play tennis on a clay court. They walked through paths cut into the back acreage. And just before he left, he jumped into the pool with all his clothes on. It would keep him cool on the way back home, he said. She laughed.

That summer, Joseph came every day – except the weekends, when Madeleine's parents were home. They watched movies, they played tennis on clay courts, they walked long walks through the back acreage, and they swam in the pool. She laughed and sometimes he laughed too. She never asked him why his face looked so beat up. He didn't tell her what his father was doing to him because he wasn't around anymore to carry the tools.

That fall, she went away to school in Andover.

It nearly killed Joseph.

He went to the library computers every afternoon to write to her. Writing stunk, but it was better than nothing.

A little better than nothing.

She came back home for Thanksgiving and Joseph walked seven miles to see her on the stormy, icy Friday afterwards.

The nanny answered the door.

'Aren't you the plumber's boy?' she said.

Joseph said he was. Was Madeleine home?

The nanny looked at him. 'Go away before you get yourself into a lot of trouble you don't want.' She closed the door.

Joseph walked home, seven miles.

On Sunday, Madeleine went back to her school in Andover.

She came home again for Christmas break. On the first Monday, Joseph walked seven miles. It was cold and snowy and Joseph's coat was too small. But he walked seven miles and knocked at her door.

This time, Madeleine answered, and she held out her hands.

She brought him inside. She had hot chocolate and he had coffee in the kitchen. They sat by the fire and talked and talked and talked. They went outside – Joseph used the gardener's old coat – and they walked through the quiet snowy acreage, holding hands. Madeleine threw snowballs at him and hit him sometimes. He threw snowballs too, but he never hit her. Not once. He couldn't even imagine hitting Madeleine with a snowball.

Because he loved her.

He loved her.

He had never known love before.

He had never known how much it could fill him.

He had never known anything, he thought.

Behind the acreage, they walked along a frozen river

and Madeleine pretended she was skating. She was beautiful beyond beautiful, even skating in her boots. The sun went down and she skated in her boots, and skated, and skated, and Joseph watched her until the sky was dark and Jupiter was up and Joseph pointed to it: 'It's my favourite planet,' he said. And she held his arm and looked at Jupiter and she said, 'Mine too – now.'

When they got back from the snowy woods, the nanny's car was in the driveway.

Madeleine told him to keep the coat and Joseph walked home, seven miles.

Madeleine's Christmas break lasted for three weeks. Joseph came every day, except for the weekends.

On the weekends, he stayed home and thought about Madeleine until everything in him would almost burst.

He had never known.

How could he have known?

On the day before Madeleine had to go back to Andover, Joseph walked seven miles to her house in a rain that was mostly sleet, and the gardener's jacket did just about nothing to keep him warm. He was soaked and shivering when Madeleine opened the door. She brought him over to the fire and found him a red woollen blanket and what was he thinking he could die in weather like this, and he got out of his wet things and wrapped himself in the red woollen blanket and sat close to the fire while she made hot chocolate and coffee. She brought the mugs in and they sat together and Madeleine asked Joseph what he remembered about his mother and he said he remembered going outside with her after a storm and pouring boiling maple syrup onto new snow and then eating it.

That afternoon, while Joseph's things were drying, they boiled maple syrup and Joseph put on the gardener's boots and they took the pan outside. They found new snow and they ladled the syrup onto the powder, and when it froze – sort of – Joseph picked it up and fed it to Madeleine, and Madeleine picked it up and fed it to Joseph, and she smeared some on his mouth and she laughed and she leaned forwards and she kissed him for the first time.

The first time.

Then they went back inside, under the red woollen blanket.

The nanny found them later, and the trouble she had predicted began.

She said she wasn't going to be held responsible and she wasn't going to lose her job over this. No, sir, she wasn't.

But she did.

Madeleine's parents took out an injunction against Joseph. A policeman delivered it. Joseph was to have no contact at all with Madeleine. Any violation meant he would be prosecuted to the fullest extent of the law. The very fullest extent.

Then the State of Maine * Department of Health and Human Services delivered their news: Joseph and his father would begin receiving monthly visits and evaluations.

And Madeleine was withdrawn from her school in Andover and sent to a school in western Pennsylvania. Joseph did not know which one.

Three months later, the Department of Health and Human Services visited Joseph's father while Joseph was at school. Mrs Stroud told him that Madeleine Joyce was pregnant. She was still only thirteen years old. Based upon this new information and Mrs Stroud's observations, the DHHS had decided to remove Joseph from his home and to place him in a juvenile facility for boys. Mr Brook should know that his son might face criminal charges.

'Wouldn't be the first time,' said Joseph's father to Mrs Stroud. 'And probably not the last.'

Mrs Stroud was waiting for Joseph when he came home from school.

His father said, 'Hey, stud, you got some girl—'

'Joseph,' Mrs Stroud said, 'I want to talk with you about Madeleine.'

Afterwards he packed. He was sort of numb. He was going to be a father. A father! He was thirteen! A father.

He was going to be a father!

And he knew he had to be with Madeleine, and they were going to have a baby, and he had to keep the baby away from his father, and that meant they would have to leave Maine.

Maybe Madeleine's parents would help them.

And that's what he asked Mrs Stroud as they drove away. Could he see Madeleine now? Would her parents help them?

For a long time, Mrs Stroud didn't say a thing.

Finally, she told him the truth.

Madeleine's parents were not going to help them. And he could not see Madeleine. She was in school in western Pennsylvania for two more months, and then she would return to New England. It was not Joseph's business where she would stay. He should forget her. He was only thirteen.

He was going to be a father, he said.

He was only thirteen, she said again.

She took him to a group home for boys.

He stayed one day and one night, and left.

Mrs Joyce called the police when he showed up at their house.

The police did not care when Joseph told them he only wanted to talk to Madeleine's parents. He only wanted them to know who he was, who he really was, so they would let him see Madeleine. He wanted them to know, he wanted them to know he loved her. After that, if they didn't want to help them with the baby, then OK, he wanted them to know they'd make it on their own. He would work. He would do whatever it took.

He loved her.

'How old are you, kid?' asked the policeman.

Joseph told them.

'You're just a baby yourself,' said the policeman.

The policeman took him back to the group home.

Joseph stayed one day and one night, and then he left.

The police found him on the Pennsylvania Turnpike, thumbing west.

They took him to Lake Adams Juvenile. With a fence around it. A very high fence. The exits were always locked.

During the night, the door to his room was locked. From the outside.

In October, Mrs Stroud came with papers.

'What are they for?' said Joseph.

'You're a minor,' said Mrs Stroud, 'and your father is still your legal guardian. But we think it's important that you, as the father, sign these papers. They involve parental rights, Joseph, which you are signing over to the state so that we can find the best possible future for your baby. And frankly, since your father is not cooperating, we need you to help us.'

That was how Joseph heard for the first time he was now a father.

He looked at the forms. The baby was a girl. Her name was Jupiter Joyce.

Joseph wept.

Mrs Stroud handed him a photograph. 'I'm really not supposed to give you this, but . . .'

The baby was beautiful. Beautiful beyond beautiful. She was holding her perfect hands and her perfect fingers and her perfect fingernails up over her head, and her tiny mouth was wide with a yawn, and her eyes were open and she was looking at him – right at him – and she was warm in a light green blanket and a light green cap and she glowed with light like the brightest planet in the darkest sky.

'Joseph,' said Mrs Stroud, 'you need to sign these papers.'

'No,' he said.

'Joseph, Jupiter has to be put up for adoption. I promise you she'll go to a good family who will love her and take care of her.'

'I love her. I'll take care of her.' He put the picture in his pocket.

'Joseph, you're barely fourteen. You can't take care of her. If you want what's best for Jupiter, you'll—'

'We're what's best for Jupiter,' said Joseph. 'Maddie and me.'

Mrs Stroud put her hand against Joseph's face. He did not move. 'Joseph, I didn't want to tell you this. I thought it would be too much. Maybe it will be too much. But you have to sign these papers. If you don't, Madeleine's parents will prosecute you.'

Joseph looked at her.

'There were complications. Joseph, Madeleine—'

'Don't say anything,' Joseph said quickly. 'Don't say anything. Don't say anything. Don't say anything. Don't—'

'Joseph, please.'

That was how Joseph heard for the first time that he would never see Madeleine again, never touch her again, never talk to her again, never walk through the woods with her again.

That was how Joseph heard for the first time that Madeleine, whom he loved, was gone.

'Madeleine would want this,' said Mr Stroud.

Quickly he signed the papers and ran back towards his room.

He stopped in the boys' bathroom. He didn't know what was coming over him, but it was huge and terrible and strong. It was inside him and outside him, and it was already starting to scream, and it was getting louder and his head was getting louder and his brain was getting louder and he threw water in his face but he couldn't stop it he couldn't stop it he couldn't stop it he couldn't stop it.

When Manny Toole came in, he said Joseph looked like he needed something bad and he could have these if he wanted them, and he held out his hand and there were two yellow pills. Joseph took them both and splashed water into his mouth and the whole world exploded and he staggered into one of the stalls and shattered there until one of the teachers found him.

Later, his hands bound behind him, they told Joseph he tried to kill the teacher.

That's when Joseph went to Stone Mountain.

He stayed one day and one night, and then he tried to leave.

At the top of the fence, his foot caught in a roll of

razor wire. When he pulled it free, the razor ripped over the top of his foot, and as he fell, the razor sliced open his side, starting from under his right arm and cutting all along to almost his knee.

The doctor said he had never put so many stitches into one boy's body before.

When Mrs Stroud came to see him, she said Madeleine was gone, so where did he think he was going?

Joseph didn't say anything.

Mrs Stroud said she couldn't help him if he wouldn't talk to her. So Joseph looked at her and said, 'Where do you think I was going?'

'Joseph,' said Mrs Stroud, 'you can't be a father when you're only fourteen.'

'I am a father,' said Joseph.

'No,' said Mrs Stroud, 'you signed away—'

'I'm Jupiter's father,' said Joseph. 'I will always be Jupiter's father.'

After that, he wouldn't talk with Mrs Stroud.

He wouldn't talk with anyone.

He lived at Stone Mountain for a month. He wouldn't talk to anyone. Not even when he got beat up. Not the first time, not the second time, not the third time. Not even when they held him down and . . .

He wouldn't talk to anyone.

After the third time, Mrs Stroud said she was going to speak with the best foster parents she knew. She couldn't promise anything. They hadn't taken in any boys for almost twelve years. They lived on an organic farm. Would he like that, living on a farm? They didn't have much technology, but they had a pond, and acres of land, and animals. What did he think?

A week later, Joseph came to Eastham. He began to milk cows.

That night, after skating on the pond under the silver moon and Jupiter, Joseph talked more than he had ever talked before altogether. It was like he had finally figured out who he wanted to tell, and once he started, he couldn't stop until he was done. It took a long time. My father and mother and I didn't say anything. We hardly moved, except my father, who had to add all the wood I had brought out to the fire. And when Joseph finished, he went up to the Big Barn, and we could hear Rosie mooing. I think he didn't want us to see him . . . you know. But it was OK if Rosie saw. It was OK for Rosie to tell Joseph that she loved him.

My father kicked out the fire. My mother held me. I said, 'Why can't he see Jupiter?' And they said I had to try to understand. Joseph was only fourteen. He couldn't be a father. Seeing Jupiter would only hurt him even more. And Jupiter might be upset, maybe even frightened.

'Suppose you're wrong?' I said. 'Suppose Jupiter wants to find Joseph?'

My mother held me even closer. My father put his hand on my back.

JOSEPH came in late that night. He got ready for bed, then stood by the window, even though the room was really cold. He looked out the panes that were already a little frosted over, and the moonlight flooded him, and his scar was a bright ragged line along his side. He leaned into the glass until his forehead touched the pane. He stood there perfectly still, the moonlight flooding him as if it would drown him. But he didn't move.

'Joseph,' I finally said, 'it's freezing.'

He didn't turn around.

'What are you looking at?'

'I can't see Jupiter,' he said. 'The moon's too bright. And I don't know where she is.'

'It's where it always is,' I said.

'No, it isn't.'

He wrapped his arms around himself. When he finally turned, I could see his breath in the moonlight.

'I'm going to find her,' he said. 'I'm not going to stay alone.'

'You're not alone.'

He shook his head.

'You're not.'

'I'm alone,' he said.

'You've got me,' I said.

He laughed, but not a happy laugh. 'Jackie, I'm a whole lifetime ahead of you,' he said. He left the window and climbed up onto the bunk.

The moonlight kept flooding into the dark.

'It's Jack,' I said.

'Yeah,' he said.

'And no, you're not,' I said.

He settled into the bed. 'OK,' he said.

I woke up again and again that night, but I didn't hear Joseph moving or breathing or dreaming. If it hadn't been for the dent his body made above me, I would have thought he was gone. Downstairs, the chimney clock chimed the quarter hours – and I heard a lot of them – until once I woke and the dent was gone and I jerked up and looked across the room.

Joseph was standing by the window again. The moon was down.

He was looking for Jupiter in the cold and the dark.

. . .

B Y morning it was snowing.

Not a lot, but enough to pile up on the branches, and the cupola on the barn, and the woodpile, and if we wanted to skate again we'd have to shovel off the ice on the pond – again. The bus was a little late, and Mr Haskell skidded the back tyres in the new snow when he stopped for us.

I guess Mr Haskell didn't like the way Joseph looked at him when he got on.

'Hey, you think you could drive a bus better, go ahead.' He leaned back and pointed to the steering wheel. 'Go ahead.'

Joseph walked past him on the way to the back.

'That's what I thought,' said Mr Haskell, and he levered the door closed and gunned the engine so the bus swayed sharply.

Joseph walked down the aisle like he was walking on a sidewalk.

I fell into Danny Nations.

'You want to try finding your own seat?' he said.

I slid behind him, next to Ernie Hupfer, who was looking out the window like it was the most important thing in the whole wide world.

'It's snow, Ernie,' I said. 'White flakes. They come down every winter. You've seen them before.'

We passed old First Congregational, Mr Haskell skidding the back tyres around for the left turn so that the Alliance Bridge came into view and then whirled out of view, like a movie camera going berserk.

We all held on.

Ernie turned to me and his face was tight.

'Listen, Jack.'

'Relax, Ernie. He's not going into the river. You won't die.'

'Just listen. Don't hang around with Psycho back there, OK?'

'What's that supposed to mean?'

'Just don't hang around with him.'

'Why?'

'No reason.'

'Ernie—'

'I said, no reason.'

Danny Nations leaned over his seat, twisting one of his ear buds. 'What's so serious back here?'

'Nothing,' said Ernie.

'I think someone's tightie-whities got a little too tightie,' said Danny.

'Shut up,' Ernie said, and went back to looking out the window.

Five

I FIGURED OUT what Ernie meant a couple of days later.

In gym class.

A Friday. When Coach Swieteck was gone to some stupid PE conference. And we had a substitute who knew as much about running a gym class as a gerbil would.

I knew when Ernie told me we had to roll up the mats at the end of class and I went to do it with him and Coach Substitute hollered, 'Hey, thanks for doing that without my asking,' and I looked at Ernie and then I looked around the gym and some of the other eighth graders were still shooting baskets but Joseph had already gone into the locker room.

Nick Porter and Brian Boss and Jay Perkins were gone too.

Ernie said, 'Jack.'

I dropped my side of the mat.

Ernie said, 'Don't,' but I did.

The way into the eighth-grade side of the locker room was blocked by stupid eighth graders standing like cows at a gate they can't get through.

I ran down the centre aisle to the other end of the locker room. Someone was slamming against the lockers and slamming again, and I heard Joseph yell something and someone else yell something, and then I got to the end of the aisle and turned in to the eighth-grade side.

Jay Perkins was on the floor, bent over and holding his nose because of all the blood coming out of it. He was hollering, but the words were sort of snotty and hard to make out.

Past him, Brian Boss and Nick Porter were both holding Joseph and slamming him again and again against the lockers.

I figured they'd worn their cups.

Beyond them, the stupid stupid stupid eighth graders stood watching. Watching as Joseph got slammed again and again.

Joseph didn't have much of his shirt left on him, and you could imagine the welts the lockers were leaving on his back. Some blood, too, but that might have been from Jay Perkins.

The look on his face? What do you think?

Until he saw me. He couldn't say anything, because Nick Porter suddenly had his hand across Joseph's jaw and he was strangling him and shoving him back into the lockers. But even so, when Joseph saw me, he shook his head.

He wanted me out of there.

Then Jay Perkins stood up.

Someone called out, 'Jay, enough,' but I don't think Jay Perkins even heard him. And if he did, he wasn't thinking it was enough.

He stood in front of Joseph. He was still hollering, but he was snarling, too. He pulled his arm back and Nick Porter took his hand away from Joseph's face and Joseph closed his eyes.

Everything stopped.

The stupid herd of eighth graders. Nick Porter and Brian Boss. Joseph. Jay Perkins with blood on his fist.

Everything stopped, and I thought I heard some of the words Joseph cried in his dreams – the words I didn't even know. I think they were coming from me.

I pushed off from the lockers, took three quick steps, and slammed into Jay Perkins's back.

His face ploughed into the wire mesh of the lockers, and he fell to his knees again.

Then the words were coming out of Jay Perkins.

And he didn't just say them. He screeched them loud

enough to be heard in whole different wings of Eastham Middle School.

And while he said what he was saying, Brian Boss turned to look at me, and Joseph brought his right knee up as hard as he could.

It turned out, Brian Boss wasn't wearing a cup after all.

He threw up all over Jay Perkins.

Then he screeched too.

And, his right arm now free, Joseph smashed his own fist into Nick Porter's face.

Again, and again, and again.

He was crying. Like at night.

He stopped only when the stupid herd of eighth graders scattered and Coach Substitute ran in to find out what all the screeching was about.

I T would have to be Mr Canton.

I sat in his office. Still in gym stuff. With some blood on me – not mine.

Two offices down, Joseph and Brian Boss and Nick Porter and Jay Perkins were in Principal Tuchman's office. You could tell that Jay Perkins was there by the smell, since he had Brian Boss's throw-up all over him.

But I was in Mr Canton's office.

And Mr Canton was standing behind his desk, probably so he wouldn't scuff up his shoes. His arms were crossed.

'So you want to tell me what a sixth grader was doing in the eighth-grade side of the locker room, in an eighth-grade fight?' he said.

'Winning,' I said.

'Don't be smart, Jackson. We've talked before about what happens when you're around Joseph Brook.'

'It was three guys on one. Three against one. What was I supposed to do?'

'For starters, go get a teacher.'

I looked at him.

'Would you have left a guy being beat up to go find a teacher?'

Mr Canton looked at me, then sat down.

'This is what I meant, Jackson.'

'Jack.'

Mr Canton nodded. 'This wasn't your fight. This wasn't about you. But look what happened. You might get suspended for fighting. All because you were hanging around Joseph Brook. I'm telling you, I know his type. Trouble follows him like a yellow dog.'

'I've seen what happens to yellow dogs,' I said. 'It was three against one.'

Mr Canton sighed. 'Yes, it was. I'm not saying you didn't think it was the right thing to do. And I'm not saying it was and I'm not saying it wasn't. The point is, you're a different kid around Joseph Brook, and not a better kid. You need to be careful around him. Maybe put some distance between you two.'

'I did think it was the right thing,' I said, 'and you

still didn't answer my question. Would you have left a guy being beat up to go find a teacher?'

Mr Canton sighed again. 'Go get clean,' he said. 'Bell rings in ten minutes.'

I did. Meanwhile, Mr Canton called my parents.

THE talk I had with Mr Canton was pretty much the talk I had with my mother and father. I needed to not get pulled into the trouble that followed Joseph, they said. I needed to remember I was in sixth grade and not in eighth grade, and I was not the hero who was supposed to be going to the rescue all the time. I needed to remember that—

'Would you have left a guy being beat up to go find a teacher?' I asked.

My father, he wiped his hand across his face, and what was left behind was a smile.

Really, a smile.

'Not in a million years,' he said.

'John!' said my mother.

'Well, he asked,' said my father. 'Just be careful, Jack. Be careful.'

My mother took my hands. 'Jack,' she said, 'you do understand that Joseph is not your—'

'I know,' I said.

My mother stood and held me. Then my father sent me out to start the milking.

They talked with Joseph next.

That night, before he turned the light out, Joseph sat on the desk. He had a few bruises darkening both his sides and some cuts on his back from the wire lockers. And his left cheek was a kind of zombie blue.

'Jackie,' he said.

'Jack.'

'Yeah. Listen, you should have stayed out of it.'

'Maybe,' I said.

'You should have.'

He jumped off the desk and turned the light out.

Against the starlight coming in the window, I saw him turn to watch for Jupiter.

'But you know what?' he said.

'What?'

'No one's ever had my back before. Except Maddie. Thanks.'

I got up and stood next to him in the dark. He pointed to Jupiter, lit up, brighter than anything else in the sky.

The air was so cold, it was chiming like a struck tuning fork. I was shivering and my feet were freezing. But I guess I was about as happy as I'd ever been.

JOSEPH and Brian Boss and Nick Porter and Jay Perkins all got four days of suspension for fighting – the last four days before Christmas vacation. The letter Mr Tuchman sent said they would be expelled if there were further incidents. And they would have to make up all their missed work once they got back to school in January. Including the PE periods.

Except Joseph didn't have to wait until January to make up all his classes.

When I got home the first Monday of Joseph's suspension, Mr D'Ulney and Mrs Halloway were just getting out of a car. You know how strange it is to see teachers at your house? You instantly feel like you must have done something you'd rather not have your parents hear about.

But they weren't there for me. They were there for Joseph.

So Mrs Halloway graded papers while Mr D'Ulney went over some proofs with Joseph and assigned his homework, and when he was done, Mr D'Ulney graded papers while Mrs Halloway went over poetic scansion, which no one really cares about, and she made me identify stressed and unstressed syllables and name their rhythms with Joseph, even though I was going to have to do it again in class the next day. But she said it would be good preparation so I should stop fussing, sit down, and get busy. And when she was done and they were getting ready to leave – she left Joseph a bunch of homework for the next day too – Coach Swieteck was pulling up in his van. Joseph and I went out, and he said, 'Show me your barn' and we went into the Big Barn and he said, 'This'll do. Go get the weights in the back of the van,' and he threw Joseph the keys. So we brought the weights into the Big Barn – four trips – and Joseph said, 'Isn't it going to be cold out here?' and Coach Swieteck said, 'It's a tough world, kiddo,' and that was that. PE for Joseph was lifting weights in the barn. For an hour. And me, too, since Coach Swieteck said it wouldn't hurt.

They came all four days of Joseph's suspension.

All four days, so he wouldn't have to make up those classes in January.

At the beginning of Christmas vacation, we saw Brian Boss and Nick Porter and Jay Perkins at the Eastham Library – not that they were in the library, but we were, since Joseph needed the second volume of *Octavian Nothing*. It had snowed pretty hard and the streets were white with packed snow. When we came out, they were driving by, Jay Perkins on his snowmobile with a face that looked like it had been smacked up against a locker – which it had – and Brian Boss behind Nick Porter on his snowmobile. They drove by slowly, watching. Joseph handed me the second volume of *Octavian Nothing* and he stood with his hands at his sides, watching back.

On the way back home, they passed us again on the road.

'You're dead, kid,' Jay Perkins hollered from his snowmobile.

Joseph handed me the second volume of *Octavian Nothing* again and we watched them until they turned out of sight. Then he looked at me. 'Don't let them get behind you, ever,' he said.

'I won't,' I said.

Then he took the book back.

It was the last time we went outside for a few days, except when we went out to the Small Barn for Quintus

Sertorius and the Big Barn to milk and to lift weights, wearing just about everything warm that we owned – including the long underwear. The weather turned even colder, the kind of cold that froze the inside of your nose as soon as you stepped out of the house, and the sound of your foot on the snow was a crunch, and you half closed your eyes against the freezing, and you held your coat tight against you. Still, there's something about coming into a barn full of warm cows, their sweet breath, the scent of the dry hay, and the sounds of their shuffling and snuffling. With the lanterns hissing, it all glows. And like I said, leaning against a warm cow during milking is fine.

The cows were always glad to see us – maybe because they had nothing else to do, closed up in the barn for the winter. Dahlia would look around and sometimes she would wink. Really. And Rosie? Now Rosie mooed whenever she heard Joseph coming into the barn. She waved her rump in delight. When he milked, she thought she was giving just for him.

And when he milked, Joseph talked about Madeleine. And when we lifted weights, Joseph talked about Madeleine. And when we carried bales of hay to Quintus Sertorius, Joseph talked about Madeleine. At supper, he talked about Madeleine. At night, in the dark before sleep, he talked about Madeleine.

How the first time he danced with Madeleine was during a snowstorm. He knew he was going to have to walk seven miles home and the snow was already darkening the afternoon. But it was warm inside, and *he* was warm inside, and they touched hands, and Madeleine laughed, and she began to hum. How they held each other and danced to Madeleine's humming, and she had her eyes closed but Joseph watched her – he didn't want to close his eyes. He didn't ever want to close his eyes. He didn't want to miss a second.

How one wintry day they duelled with long icicles that had dripped down from the roof, and how she hit his icicle again and again and clipped it down to a little nub, and how she stabbed him in the chest with her icicle and he fell down like he was dead, and suddenly she got all scared and yelled at him to get up, don't do that, get up, and he did.

How Madeleine liked to watch movies eating popcorn with cinnamon – but never butter. How Madeleine liked to read poetry and how he pretended that he did too but she knew he really didn't. How Madeleine wanted to go to MIT someday and become an engineer and travel to places that needed her, where she would dig deep wells so that no one would ever have to go without fresh water again. How Madeleine loved going barefoot. How Madeleine's teddy bear was named Bunny Beau – for no reason.

How they could be quiet with each other.

How holding her hand warmed everything in him.

How he sometimes still felt her hand.

I guess that night at the pond, while my father and mother and I got colder and colder listening to Joseph, I guess that night unfroze him.

• • •

O N Christmas Eve morning, after milking, my father and Joseph and I took a couple of bow saws and an axe just in case and headed up into the hills to find a tree – not too far, since we had to drag it back. My father and I usually argued back and forth about which one to take, but we didn't this year. For Joseph, this was the first Christmas tree he'd ever had, and when he looked at one and touched its branches and smiled – number five, sort of – it didn't seem right to argue. It was a sweet fir that cut easily, and Joseph and I each took a side, and we carried it back home and put it up in the front room.

Like every year, the smell of it meant Christmas.

My mother had brought the boxes of ornaments down from the attic, and we waited while my father fussed the lights on, and then we opened the boxes.

Every ornament, a story. The old ones from when my mother was a kid. The handmade ones from my first grade, and second grade, and third grade. The red glass bulbs my father bought my mother one Christmas. The twelve golden angels – including this year's new one – one for every year of my life. The glass bluebird with spread wings. The carolers with knitted mufflers. The silver trumpet, the cockeyed teddy bear with his red and white scarf, the tiny sled packed with tinier toys.

When we were almost finished, my mother went out into the kitchen and brought back a small box. 'This one's for you,' she said to Joseph, 'for your first Christmas with us,' and she handed him the box.

Another golden angel.

Joseph took it out of the tissue paper. He hung it on the tree and pushed it a little with his finger. It turned and glittered with the lights. 'Jupiter would love this,' he said.

We milked a little early on Christmas Eve afternoon, since Christmas Eve at night and Easter in the morning are the two times my mother is going to have us at new First Congregational 'even if the Gates of Hell stand against us,' she said. That meant we ate early and scrubbed long – Joseph, too. Afterwards she inspected us – especially the zombie blue patch on Joseph's left cheek – and while she inspected, she asked Joseph if he'd ever been to a Congregational church service before, and he said he hadn't ever been to any church service before, Congregational or not.

My mother looked at him.

'Never once?' she said.

He shook his head.

'Didn't your mother—' And immediately she knew she'd gone too far, since Joseph backed up against the wall and looked down. 'I'm sorry, Joseph. I'm being nosy and I hate nosy people. I'll finish the dishes. You and Jack run upstairs and get ready. There are two pressed shirts for you on the banister. And, Jack, this year you can't wear your work boots to church. No argument. Nope, don't even try.'

I didn't wear my work boots.

The night was cold and dark when we got to new

First Congregational, and the stars were as thick as cream. Inside, the air was pretty thick too, filled with that sweet waxy smell of candles burning. We were a little late and the pews were mostly filled, so we sat up close to the front, where we could pretty much look right into the manger. Past the red and blue plaster figures, a pink baby lay mostly naked in the hay – as if anyone would leave a mostly naked new baby in hay. We sang 'Hark! The Herald Angels Sing' and 'O Little Town of Bethlehem' and 'O Come, All Ye Faithful' – the ones you'd expect, I guess. But Joseph didn't sing – maybe because he never sang, or maybe because he didn't know the songs.

And then Reverend Ballou got up to tell the story.

About Joseph and Mary, two kids, really, not married, who found out they were going to have a baby. They were in trouble, and they knew it, and there was no one to help them, and plenty of people who didn't want to help them. But angels came and told them not to be afraid because God would be with them. And the baby would be special. And Joseph wasn't afraid anymore. He took care of Mary, and when they had to go to a faraway city and couldn't find a nice place to stay – because, like I said, there sure wasn't anyone helping them – Joseph found a place and that's where they had their baby. And the star that shone over them that night led others to them, and they knew the baby was special too. And Joseph and Mary loved the child, and when they went back home, they remembered everything that happened and they treasured it in their hearts.

In the pew, Joseph didn't move the whole time. Not a muscle.

When the service was over and we had finished 'Joy to the World,' Joseph handed me the hymnal and I put it in the rack and followed my mother and father out into the aisle. But Joseph didn't leave the pew with us. He was staring at the manger, past the red plaster Joseph and the blue plaster Mary, at the mostly naked child in the hay.

We waited for him while the church emptied out.

We were just about the last ones to leave. Reverend Ballou took Joseph's hand to shake it, and Joseph said, 'How much of that story is true?'

Reverend Ballou considered this.

'I think it all has to be true, or none of it,' he said.

'The angels?' said Joseph. 'Really?'

'Why not?' said Reverend Ballou.

'Because bad things happen,' said Joseph. 'If there were angels, then bad things wouldn't happen.'

'Maybe angels aren't always meant to stop bad things.'

'So what good are they?'

'To be with us when bad things happen.'

Joseph looked at him.

'Then where the hell were they?' he said.

I thought Reverend Ballou was going to start bawling.

And that was the end of our Christmas Eve service at new First Congregational.

O N Christmas morning, it was snowing hard – again. We milked first – since cows don't celebrate Christmas – and then came in to a breakfast of eggs and grapefruit and cherry babka and hot tea. And afterwards, the presents.

The usual stuff. Wool socks for Joseph and me. And wool shirts. New jeans. New boots. A new Barlow knife for me, a new Buck knife for Joseph. Books – pretty good, except Joseph got a copy of *Walden*, which looked about as boring as wool socks.

When it was over and we sat back, Joseph reading the first page of *Walden* – probably to be polite – my father said, 'Joseph, I think there's one more thing.'

Joseph looked at him.

My father pointed to the tree.

There was an envelope underneath Joseph's angel.

Joseph stood up and took it. He opened it slowly. He unfolded the paper. He read it, and then read it again, out loud.

'"We'll help,"' he read.

'Help with what?' I said.

'We'll call Mrs Stroud tomorrow and see if we can set up a meeting,' my mother said.

Then I knew.

But I think Joseph knew what they meant right away.

He put the paper back into the envelope. He slipped the envelope between the pages of *Walden*. And no kidding, watching him, I thought he was going to start bawling, just like Reverend Ballou.

He walked over to my mother and she put her arms around him and he put his arms around her and he leaned into her – the way he did with Rosie.

Then my father came up behind him. He put his hand on Joseph's back.

Christmas is the season for miracles, you know. Sometimes they come big and loud, I guess – but I've never seen one of those. I think probably most miracles are a lot smaller, and sort of still, and so quiet, you could miss them.

I didn't miss this one.

When my father put his hand on Joseph's back, Joseph didn't even flinch.

Six

IT STAYED WICKED cold all through Christmas vacation. Ten or twelve below zero every morning, and when it warmed up to zero or so in the afternoon, it snowed. Joseph and I shovelled by the house and the barns, and shovelled and shovelled and shovelled, and we had to throw the snow higher and higher to make it over the drifts. Every day after Christmas, it was more snow. And when we went outside on the first day of the new year, again, we had four or five new inches to shovel off the paths – except this time, when we were almost all done and I was throwing one last full load, I suddenly felt a shovelful scatter across my back, and when I turned around, another shovelful across my chest and in my face, and Joseph was smiling and laughing.

Joseph was smiling and laughing.

Number six – not even sort of.

So, what would you do? I pulled a shovelful from a drift and threw it at him – and missed. So another shovelful, and I chased him until we got almost to the Big Barn – he was laughing so hard, he was doubled over – and I threw it onto his back. And then of course he had to get another shovelful and I had to get one and . . . You can figure out the rest.

We spent a long time shoveling out in front of the house and barns – again.

The cows were annoyed when we came in a little late for milking. Dahlia stepped on my foot, and when cows do that, they mean to.

But it was the first time Joseph had played.

And laughed.

It was worth an annoyed cow.

Supper was fine that night. Chicken, carrots, and sweet potatoes, bread pudding with homemade vanilla ice cream and homemade chocolate sauce. We were all laughing about the snow, and how it was coming down again, and how there would be a lot more shovelling tomorrow and maybe we'd have to do it twice again.

Joseph had played!

Then the phone rang and immediately everything stopped.

Since Christmas, my parents had been waiting for the call about Jupiter.

Joseph, too.

He stood frozen. His chair fell back and he bent down to pick it up but he looked at my mother the whole time. And she looked at him.

She got up and answered the phone.

It wasn't Mrs Stroud. And it wasn't about Jupiter.

It was Joseph's father.

'Hello, Mr Brook,' said my mother.

Joseph backed up against the wall.

My mother listened for a long time. She wasn't listening happily.

'I don't think that's possible,' she said.

She listened again for a long time.

'Has Mrs Stroud been informed? We won't allow this unless—'

More listening.

'All right,' she said. 'Not before four o'clock. Yes, four o'clock.'

More listening.

'All right,' she said. 'If that's what's been decided. Yes, he's right here. I suppose you can talk to him.'

She looked at Joseph and held the phone out. He came away from the wall and took it.

'Yeah,' he said.

My mother sat down at the table. 'Joseph's father has hired a lawyer,' she said.

'OK,' said Joseph.

'He's somehow gotten visitation rights. I don't know how, since . . .' She looked at me and stopped. 'Anyway, he says he'll be here on Monday to see Joseph.'

'We'll need to talk to Mrs Stroud first,' said my father.

'OK,' said Joseph.

'You bet we will,' said my mother.

'I'm OK,' said Joseph.

'No,' said Joseph.

'OK,' said Joseph. 'OK.'

He hung up the phone and sat down.

'You all right?' said my father.

Joseph nodded.

'Joseph, if you don't want . . .'

Joseph stood up. 'I'm going to check on Rosie one more time,' he said. 'I don't remember if I filled her hay bin.'

'We did,' I said.

'I'm just going to check,' said Joseph.

He went down the hall. When he opened the back door, a cold wind blew in.

That cold wind stayed with us as we waited for Joseph to come back inside. And even after he did, it stayed with us the rest of that night. And it stayed with us the rest of Christmas vacation. Joseph didn't play anymore. We didn't talk about his father coming, but it was like that feeling you have in dreams, when something is on its way and there's nothing you can do about it except to hope you wake up before it comes.

Sometimes you do.

Joseph was waiting for me after school on Monday. It was a blue day, a few high clouds, somewhere in the low teens – almost like a thaw. Joseph said he was going to walk home, and I said I'd walk with him, and he didn't say I was being a jerk. He hunched his coat together and we started off. When the bus passed, Ernie Hupfer, John Wall, and Danny Nations and his ear buds were watching out their windows, and Ernie Hupfer was shaking his head – like I really was being a jerk.

We stopped at old First Congregational and threw snowballs up at the bell. It doesn't sound the same as a good clang with a rock, but Joseph wanted to throw a bunch up there, and we did. Then we walked out to the Alliance bridge and threw snowballs into the river through the broken slats. And then Joseph said it was getting colder and I said I was still OK but he said we'd better go, and we did.

We got home a little after four o'clock.

A van was parked in the driveway. BROOK PLUMBING, it read on the side.

And a car. STATE OF MAINE ∗ DEPARTMENT OF HEALTH AND HUMAN SERVICES, it read on the side.

We went into the house, me first.

My parents were there, standing. And Mrs Stroud, standing. And Joseph's father, sitting.

'Hey, stud,' he said.

'Hey,' said Joseph.

Joseph looked down at the floor as he walked across the kitchen and laid his backpack on the counter.

'It takes a lawyer to see my own son,' said Mr Brook. 'But I finally got one. A good one.'

'OK,' said Joseph.

Mr Brook stood up.

'Let's go talk,' he said.

Joseph nodded.

'The living room's free,' said my father. He pointed. 'Right in there.'

'I'm taking my son for a drive,' said Mr Brook.

'Nope,' said Mrs Stroud. 'You'll stay here in the house.'

'Like hell we will.'

Mrs Stroud took out her phone and began hitting numbers. 'I'm about to end this visit right now, Mr Brook. Your choice.' She held her finger over the last number and looked at him.

Mr Brook looked back at Mrs Stroud, then walked over to Joseph and put his hand on Joseph's back and shoved him a little towards the living room.

You know what happened when Mr Brook put his hand on Joseph's back?

Joseph flinched.

But he went into the living room with his father anyway.

Mrs Stroud put her phone back in her purse. 'I'm sorry about this,' she said. 'I'm really very sorry. I advised against it, but he's right – he's got a good lawyer. Well, not a good lawyer. A persistent and threatening lawyer. And unfortunately, those are the ones who get exactly what they want.'

'What does he want?' said my father.

Mrs Stroud shook her head. 'I think it's money.'

'He's here for money?'

'He's complicating any adoption for Jupiter,' said Mrs Stroud. 'His lawyer claims that since Joseph is a minor, he had no parental rights to sign away. His father, his legal guardian, has those rights. And it seems that Mr Brook won't sign away anything until a large cheque arrives at his house with Madeleine's parents' signature on it. Of course, there's nothing in writing that says all this. But everyone knows that's what he's waiting for.'

My father stood up.

'So Joseph . . .'

'Mr Brook's lawyer is thinking ahead. He wants to be able to demonstrate Mr Brook's strong parental affection for his son and, by extension, his granddaughter.'

'And the girl . . .'

'Her adoption is in limbo. Madeleine's parents want to move on, and they want Jupiter adopted into a good home. But until Mr Brook signs – or stops his delays – that can't happen. No family will choose a child whose adoption might be contested.'

'Joseph's voice doesn't count?'

'He's a minor,' said Mrs Stroud.

My father and mother looked at each other. Then they looked towards the living room, where we could hear mostly Mr Brook's voice.

'Jack,' said my father, 'maybe you'd better get started on the milking. I'm not sure if Joseph is going to be—'

'OK,' I said.

It was warmer in the Big Barn, the smell of hay and old wood and leather and cow – like always. I walked past Rosie and she looked up, then back down. I guess she was disappointed I wasn't Joseph. So I started with Dahlia, and I leaned into her and listened to the rhythm of the milk into the pail.

No matter what is going on, there's something good about the rhythm of streaming milk, and the warm smell of it, and Dahlia's mooing, and the sounds of her chewing.

Except it isn't so good when you're about to finish and then you hear Mr Brook's voice again from inside your house, all the way across the yard – more annoyed than Dahlia ever thought to be.

I poured the milk into the cooler and went in.

No one looked up when I opened the door. They were all pretty much eyeball to eyeball with each other.

Joseph was standing with his back against the wall.

'A father's got rights to his own son, you know,' said Mr Brook.

'Who do you think you are, keeping him from me?' said Mr Brook.

'Now I've got a lawyer too,' said Mr Brook.

'You think I'm going to give in to someone just because they're rich?' said Mr Brook.

Mrs Stroud said, 'If you don't leave immediately, I'll . . .'

Mr Brook came closer to my father. 'And who do you think you're kidding? You know you've got a sweet deal going. You get your cheque from the state every month to keep my kid. You're in this for the money.' He pointed to Joseph. 'Does he know that?' He turned to Joseph. 'You know you're just a job for them? You are nothing but income.'

My father walked across the kitchen to the desk in the hallway. He opened a drawer and pulled out some papers. He brought them in and stood next to Joseph.

'Joseph,' he said, 'your father's right: every month, a cheque comes from the state. I want you to see where it goes.' He held out the papers. 'This is a printout from the bank. It shows cheques being put into an account every month, starting here, the first month you came to us. You see? And here's the balance in the account, every single one of the cheques added up together. You see that too?'

Joseph nodded.

'Now look here. You see your name? The account is in your name. That money is yours. We haven't taken a dime. It's for you.'

'It's the beginning of your college fund, Joseph,' said my mother.

Joseph took the printout and stared at it.

'College fund!' said Mr Brook. 'You think Joe is going to college? Like he's going to Harvard College and strut around like he's all smart and everything? Smarter than his dad? You think that's what's going to happen?'

'Yes,' said my mother. 'That's exactly what's going to happen. Joseph is going to college. And if you asked any of his teachers, they'd say so too.'

Mr Brook laughed. 'Then they don't know what for. But I do. And I'm telling you, the day's not far off when I come back here to take my son away. Like I said, a father's got rights.'

'We'll see,' said Mrs Stroud.

'We'll see?' said Mr Brook. Then he looked at me, pointed, and turned back to my parents. 'How'd you like it if someone came to take your boy away? Huh? How would you like it? I bet you'd do whatever it took to get him back. I bet you would.'

Mr Brook laughed again, then walked over to me and took me by my shoulder.

'Don't touch him,' said Joseph quickly.

Mr Brook's hand was hard and heavy, and it squeezed into my shoulder bone.

My father was coming across the room just as he lifted it.

He laughed again. 'See what I mean?' he said.

My father stood very close to him. Mrs Stroud took out her phone again.

Mr Brook turned back to Joseph. 'I'll get you out of here quick as I can. Then things will be better. I promise. It will be a whole new life for us both. And you won't have to go to college for it.'

He found his coat on the rack and opened the door.

'And, Joe,' he said, 'next time you try to tell me not to do something . . .'

He didn't finish – but he left.

It got a whole lot colder in the kitchen than in the Big Barn with the cows.

And quieter.

'I guess I'd better get back to milking,' I said.

Joseph walked across the kitchen. He found his coat too, and we went out together.

He didn't talk at all.

When Rosie heard us, she turned her head back and mooed her happy moo and waggled her rump to tell Joseph she loved him. Cows can be like that when you need them to be. Not always, but sometimes. And maybe Rosie knew Joseph needed her to be like that right then.

So she mooed her happy moo again, and Joseph rubbed her rump, and he settled the pail beneath her and leaned against her side, and he began to milk, slow and sure, the way he did.

He didn't talk the whole time, except to Rosie.

He didn't talk at supper until dessert, when in the middle of a quiet moment, he looked at my mother and said, 'Am I really going to go to college?'

My mother passed him another bowl of her canned peaches. 'I think Mr D'Ulney and Mrs Halloway would have our heads if you didn't go to college, Joseph,' she said.

Joseph smiled – sort of. I think it was the seventh time.

THE next day, the cold broke. It wouldn't last long, my father predicted, maybe a few days. The sun was out and the sky too bright a blue to look at as the snow melted off the yews and came clumping down. The cows were as restless as spring, thinking there might be new grass out in the fields, even though the snow was still pretty deep. And Quintus Sertorius would not stay in his stall, so after school Joseph and I took him out to the paddock to let him walk around. He ploughed through snow way past his knees, with both Joseph and me riding him – Joseph's first time on a horse, and bareback to boot – and Quintus Sertorius snorted and nickered and swished his tail high and did everything he could to tell us how happy he was that spring was coming, even though it was still a long way off.

Sometimes it's like that. You know something good is coming, and even though it's not even close yet, still, just knowing it's coming is enough to make you snort and nicker. Sort of.

I think just knowing my parents were going to help made Joseph believe something good was coming. Even if his father had a good lawyer. And rights.

My parents would help Joseph see Jupiter.

And someday, Joseph would go to college.

BUT the days dragged on, and they grew heavy with snow again.

The days dragged on, and they grew heavy with cold again.

The days dragged on, and they grew heavy with waiting.

My parents called Joseph's counselor twice, then three times, and she said she would like a few weeks to evaluate Joseph before she made the decision about him seeing Jupiter.

When my parents called Mrs Stroud, she said she would have to meet with Joseph's counselor first and get her opinion, and when my mother said that they had been trying to get his counselor to give her opinion, Mrs Stroud said her hands were tied and we would have to be patient.

When my parents called Joseph's teachers and asked them to write letters about Joseph's progress in their classes, Mr D'Ulney and Mrs Halloway and Coach Swieteck all wrote letters right away, but Mrs Stroud said they would have to be assembled into a file and presented to someone else in the Department of Health and Human

Services, and that the someone else was very, very busy and it might be some time before he could make a decision.

Mrs Stroud tried to explain this one afternoon to Joseph. In our kitchen. With my parents.

I was out in the barn. Milking. Of course.

But when Joseph came into the Big Barn, I could pretty much tell what Mrs Stroud had told him.

'Did she say when you can see Jupiter?' I said.

Waited a long time while he set the bucket beneath Rosie.

'Nope,' said Joseph, finally.

'Did she say how long until they decide?'

'Nope,' said Joseph.

Waited another long time. I finished Dahlia off.

'Did she say anything?' I said.

'Jupiter's in Brunswick,' Joseph said.

'Brunswick?'

'Yeah.'

He got to work on Rosie.

'Brunswick is south of here, right?' he said.

'Joseph, you're not . . .'

'South, right?'

'Yeah, but you can't—'

'Jackie, let's just shut up for now, OK?'

'OK,' I said.

'OK,' he said.

I poured the milk into the cooler.

'It's Jack,' I said.

'Yeah,' said Joseph.

Then we shut up. Both of us.

We didn't talk at supper. Or through homework that night. We didn't talk when I went to bed and Joseph stood in the cold dark, watching for Jupiter. Or at breakfast. Or on the bus. In any of our classes.

We didn't talk at all.

And I don't think Joseph talked to anyone else, either.

At the end of the day, when I went out to meet him by the school bus and he wasn't there, I figured he was walking home so he didn't have to talk. I got on the bus and watched for him the whole way, past the turn by old First Congregational, past the Alliance bridge, all along the frozen Alliance.

I never saw him.

And when I got home, he wasn't there.

'Where's Joseph?' my mother said.

'I think he might be walking,' I said.

She suddenly looked worried. 'I suppose that's it,' she said. But she went out to the road to watch for him. Then after a few minutes, she went to the barns to find my father.

At milking time, Joseph still wasn't home. 'I guess I'll ride into town,' said my father. 'Jack, you get started. I'm sure Joseph will be along.'

He wasn't, and an hour later, my father drove back. My mother was waiting at the door.

They went up to our room.

Some of Joseph's clothes were missing. And *Walden*. And the second volume of *Octavian Nothing*. He must have stuffed them all in his backpack that morning.

'I think I'd better call Mrs Stroud,' said my mother, and she went downstairs.

'Jack,' said my father, 'you done with the milking?'

I nodded.

'Rosie, too?'

I nodded.

He looked up at the sky, where snow clouds were lowering down like granite slabs.

'Then let's you and me get in the pickup. We'll see if we can find him.'

And I said, 'I think I know where he's going.'

My father looked at me.

'He's going to find Jupiter,' I said.

He nodded. 'Go tell your mother we'll be late for supper.'

Seven

WE WEREN'T MORE than ten minutes out of Eastham before it began to snow – and not just a little. The snow came down with hard gusts, socking the sides of the pickup and blotting out the windshield. The sound of the wind was awful, like it was crying and lost and scared and not sure what to do except to wail.

Which is sort of what I thought Joseph would be like right now, out in the middle of it – except he would never in a million years wail.

We looked out at the sides of the road, hoping we'd see Joseph trying to hitch. But now it was so dark, and the snow so hard, and the roads already getting bad, I don't think either of us had much hope. 'He's probably found a place to stay,' said my father.

I'm not sure he believed it. But what else could we believe?

Unless we believed Jay Perkins was out on his snow-mobile with Brian Boss and Nick Porter, and they had found Joseph. But neither of us said that.

The snow got thicker and thicker, and forty-five minutes outside of Eastham, we turned around. We hadn't gotten very far, but we weren't going to get much farther in this.

OK, so I was crying on the way back. My father rubbing my shoulder. Maybe he was crying too.

At home, my mother fussed with the late supper. Pancakes, since they were easy to keep warm. She had already called Mrs Stroud. Mrs Stroud had already called the police, who I guess had already called Eastham

Middle, as if Joseph might be hiding out in the janitor's closet or something. So of course Mr Canton had already come by, so full of himself, my mother said, all about how he knew something like this would happen, and kids who come from Stone Mountain are bound to run off, and it's not our fault, it's just that's who Joseph Brook is.

'I thought,' my mother said, 'I was going to take this skillet to his face.' She was holding the skillet high over her shoulder, holding it with both hands, when she said this.

My mother, I should tell you, is a pacifist. She got arrested three times during college for protesting foreign policy in El Salvador. She got arrested five times for protesting against nuclear power. So she doesn't like pushy policemen very much, or pushy vice principals, and probably Mr Canton was in more danger of a flattened face than he understood.

We waited for a phone call and listened to the storm and waited for a phone call and listened to the storm. Mugs of hot coffee and hot chocolate. My parents talking about what they should have done, how they should have known. Wondering where Joseph had found shelter. Wondering if someone had picked him up. If he was OK. If he was lost.

My parents never asked about my homework – I couldn't have done it anyway.

Later than usual, I went upstairs. The room was as cold as it ever had been. The wood floor was freezing. But for a while, in the dark, I wrapped my arms around myself and stood by the desk and looked out the window for Jupiter.

In the storm, I couldn't see a thing. Joseph wouldn't be able to either. And I wondered if Joseph knew that what he wanted, he couldn't have.

Madeleine.

Jupiter.

I wonder if he knew it couldn't be.

Maybe he didn't want to know it couldn't be.

So he was out somewhere in the snow, heading to Brunswick, when it was already too late, which he probably already knew, but he was going to Brunswick anyway.

Things go through your mind when you're standing in the cold, in the dark, watching the snow, with your feet freezing on the wood floor. They do.

THE next day, Mrs Stroud called after morning milking. No sign yet. The police had been alerted between Eastham and Brunswick. State troopers were watching on the highways and even the main back roads. They all had the picture of Joseph when he first went to Stone Mountain, even though it didn't look much like him anymore because my mother would never let him keep his hair that long. Mrs Stroud said everyone was confident he'd be found soon.

My mother said, 'It's still snowing. He won't be out on the roads.'

My father said, 'Maybe he'll find someone to help.'

And I said, 'It's Joseph. He'll know they're looking for him. He's not going to ask someone for help.'

They were quiet a long while.

We heard the school bus clanking and huffing to a stop out on the road. I didn't move. No one said anything.

The bus clanked and huffed away.

We waited.

No phone call all morning.

Or in the afternoon.

Or at night, when the snow finally stopped and Jupiter came out, bright bright bright.

The next morning, Mrs Stroud called again. No sign yet. The police were taking care of things. They would find him soon.

'That's what she told us yesterday,' said my mother, still holding the phone.

'Tell her we're wondering if we should go down to Brunswick ourselves,' said my father.

'We think we should go down to Brunswick ourselves,' said my mother into the phone.

Mrs Stroud did not think we should go to Brunswick. She was concerned we were getting too involved and had lost a little bit of perspective about Joseph Brook. After he was found, maybe we should reevaluate—

'Thank you, Mrs Stroud,' my mother said. She hung up the phone. She looked at the two of us. 'We're going down to Brunswick,' she said.

My father looked at her.

I already had my coat on.

MAYBE Joseph had found a ride all the way down to Brunswick, but we couldn't be sure, so my father stopped everyplace that looked like Joseph might have tried to stay overnight: gas stations, fast food restaurants, real food restaurants, motels, churches, even bars. The only picture we had of Joseph was of him standing next to Rosie, and it was better of Rosie than of Joseph, but it was all we had, and my mother showed it wherever we stopped.

Outside Lewiston, we found our first bit of hope in a little Baptist church set back from the road in a bunch of tall pines. Pastor Greenleaf opened the door to our knocking and he stood with one hand on his mop – he'd been cleaning the lobby tiles for Sunday – and looked at the picture, said, 'Yup,' and handed the picture back.

'Yup?' I said.

'Yup, as in "Yup, he was here."'

'When?' said my mother.

'I can't say when exactly he got here, but I found him yesterday morning on the couch in the Teen Sunday School room.'

'Is he still here?' I said.

Pastor Greenleaf shook his head. 'We had breakfast, we talked. He was pretty hungry, since I think all he'd eaten was the potato chips he found in the church kitchen – and they'd been there a lot longer than they should have been. I asked where he was from. He said Portland. I asked him to give me his parents' phone number, and I ended up calling the phone of some real estate agent in Yarmouth. When I came back, he was gone.'

'You call the police?' said my father.

'I did,' he said.

'Really?' I said.

'They told us they hadn't heard a thing,' said my mother.

'Well, they heard me,' said Pastor Greenleaf. 'What's the boy's real name?'

'Joseph Brook,' I said.

'And your name?'

'Jack.'

'Then I'll be praying for Joseph Brook. And for you, too, Jack Brook.'

'Hurd. Jackson Hurd,' said my mother.

Pastor Greenleaf looked at me. 'The boy isn't your brother?' he said.

'I have his back,' I said.

W E drove through Lewiston and down towards Brunswick. We stopped again and again and again, but no one else had seen anything of Joseph. We ate hamburgers at a diner – they hadn't seen Joseph either – and then we drove into town. Parked on Maine Street. Got out and looked around. Walked towards the statue of Joshua Lawrence Chamberlain, since it seemed a lucky thing to do. Then stood there in a cold wind, looking around and wondering what to do next.

No one else was on the street, it was that cold.

The sky spitting snow.

Clouds still granite.

'Let's split up,' I said.

My father considered this. 'OK,' he said. 'But we're not going to stay out in this cold too long.' He looked at his watch. 'And we have to be back by four thirty for milking. That gives us a couple of hours.'

He handed me Joseph's picture.

'You take that side of the street,' he said. 'We'll take the other.'

But after just a couple of blocks, I didn't.

If I were Joseph, I thought, I wouldn't go into stores. I'd walk around a neighbourhood, hope someone came out, ask if they'd heard about a new baby around – something like that. He'd make up a story about why he wanted to know, and someone would tell him, because Joseph wanted to see Jupiter so badly, they would be able to see he loved her. And that would be enough.

I turned down a block of houses.

The wind, of course, was right in my face now.

Still no one out on the street.

Clouds racking up.

A few cars driving by, probably with their heaters going full blast.

The smell of smoke from the wood stoves the families in all of these houses were gathered around.

A church bell tolling once, the sound hard as iron in the cold air.

OK, so maybe I was a little angry at Joseph by this time. I couldn't even feel my toes. Or the ends of my fingers. What chance did he have of walking around Brunswick and finding a house with a baby, and that baby would be Jupiter? I mean, what chance did he really have?

And what chance did I have of walking around the streets of Brunswick and suddenly running into him? Like, I'd turn a corner and there he'd be, watching the house where Jupiter was sleeping. What chance did either of us really have?

I walked around for an hour and a half. I saw four other people on the sidewalks, cross-armed, shoulders into the wind – they were too bundled up for me to see their faces, but none of them was Joseph-shaped. I saw two kids younger than me working on a snowman, except it was so cold, the snow wasn't packing and it looked more like a snow heap with branches sticking out for arms. An ambulance sirened past. A police car right after it. Once a car pulled into a driveway ahead of me and parents got out, and kids. The trunk popped and they all grabbed bags of groceries. The mother looked at me and almost said something, but one of the kids called and she was gone.

By the time I saw the library, I think my face had frosted to ice.

Libraries are terrific in a whole lot of ways, but one way is that on a frozen day in a Maine winter, you can go inside. I stood in the lobby for a long time, dripping and thawing. Then I wandered in. Everything was so warm. The shelves of books, the wooden tables, the bright carpets. Old people reading newspapers and staying warm. Fewer old people fussing at computers they didn't get and staying warm. A Teen Read section that didn't have enough M. T. Anderson, but it was warm. A kids' section where a whole bunch of mothers with little kids were listening to *One Morning in Maine* on tape, and they were warm. Some of the mothers held babies.

Yeah, I thought he might be there too.

But he wasn't.

I showed the picture to one of the librarians.

She didn't recognize him.

'What's his name?' she said.

'Joseph,' I said.

She showed it to another librarian.

She didn't recognize him either.

'What's he doing in Brunswick?' the second librarian asked, not even looking at me.

'Looking for his daughter,' I said.

She held the picture closer. 'His daughter?' she said.

'Her name is Jupiter,' I said.

Then she looked at me.

'What did you say?'

'Her name is Jupiter.'

She looked down at the picture again.

'This is Jupiter's father?' she said.

Remember what I said about your heart forgetting to beat?

'Joseph Brook,' I whispered.

'He's just a baby himself,' she said.

'He's fourteen.'

'Like I said.' She handed the picture back to me.

'You know her,' I said. 'You know where she is.'

'I think we'd better make a phone call,' she said.

'All he wants to do is see her. That's all. He just wants to see his daughter.'

'And who are you, exactly?'

'I have his back. Can't you let him see her?'

'You don't even know where he is.'

'When I do, can he see her?'

She looked at me. 'Listen, Guy Who Has Jupiter's Father's Back, probably not. It wouldn't be good for him, and I'm not sure it would be good for her.'

'She's four months old,' I said.

'They're not going to be together,' she said. 'Joseph Brook has to understand that. He's in high school. He can't give her what she needs.'

'He's in middle school.'

'Even worse,' she said.

'He can love her.'

The librarian looked at me, and I thought she was going to cry – just like Reverend Ballou again.

Maybe she thought I was going to cry.

Maybe I was.

'Yes, he can love her,' she said. 'He can do that. But he can't love her just for himself. He has to love her for her, too. That means he has to learn to let her live the life that can come to her with a new home.'

'He only wants to see her,' I said.

'I know,' she said. 'I really do know.'

'You're her foster mother,' I said, 'aren't you?'

She waited.

'Tell Joseph that Jupiter is doing fine,' she said. 'Tell him she's growing, and happy, and ready for a family. Tell him she needs that family. Tell him that he and his father should let her go.'

I stood there, wondering what Joseph would do if he were standing there instead of me.

'That's a lot to put on you,' she said, 'telling him that.'

I nodded.

Actually, I knew if I told him that, he'd break my nose.

'Take care of her,' I said. Nodded again. Turned to go. What else was there to do?

'Guy Who Has Jupiter's Father's Back,' she said.

I turned around.

'Tell him she's beautiful. Tell him I promise to take good care of her. And I promise she'll find a family who will love her too.'

'And tell Jupiter about Joseph,' I said. 'Tell her he tried to find her.'

'I'll tell her.'

'He tried really hard. OK?'

'OK.'

'And he loves her. He'll always love her, even if she doesn't know him.'

'I'll tell her that, too.'

I turned to go again. I had to, because I really was about to bawl.

In the Brunswick Public Library, I was about to bawl.

And that was when her phone rang.

I looked at her.

She pulled the phone out of her bag.

She listened for a minute. She was looking at me the whole time.

'OK, OK,' she said. 'Describe him to me.'

She listened.

'OK, I know who he is. Jupiter's father. No, really. He's Jupiter's father. You better make the call. I'll be right home.'

She put the phone back in the bag.

'This isn't some sort of plan, is it?'

'Plan?'

'You come where I work and he goes to the house. Did you plan that?'

'Joseph's at your house?'

'My husband says he's been walking back and forth in front of the house since noontime. If this is a plan, it's just going to get you both—'

'It's not a plan. We better go.'

She looked at me. '*We* better go? There's no "we" here. I'm going. And you better go home to wherever home is.'

I crossed my arms.

'Oh, right, you're the guy who has his back.'

'Yes,' I said. 'I'm the guy who has his back.'

She sighed. She sighed again. She looked at the other librarian, who shrugged, and she sighed again.

'OK,' she said. 'I'm going to ignore my instincts here and take you with me. But only if—'

'I'll listen to the rules in the car,' I said.

She laughed, then nodded.

'Then we better go,' she said. 'Do you mind if I drive?'

'I'm twelve,' I said.

'Never would have known,' she said, and I followed her out through the library offices and into the cold.

SHE had lots of rules.

I had to stay in the car.

My seat belt needed to be buckled even when we stopped.

I had to not interfere.

I had to not expect to see Jupiter.

I really had to not interfere.

I had to go find my parents immediately after we found Joseph.

Did I understand that I really, really had to not interfere?

We drove out from the library parking lot and down to the statue of Joshua Lawrence Chamberlain again – he looked pretty cold – and past Bowdoin College. Then we took a right down a street of houses, and let me tell you, there were a lot of cars and this was taking forever and maybe I was squirmy because she said, 'Do you have to go to the bathroom or something?' but I just kept looking out the window for Joseph.

And then, there he was. Standing in front of a smallish brick house with a yard that was probably pretty nice in the summer but was pretty bare right now. Standing with his arms crossed as if he'd wait until the end of the world.

Which he probably would.

We pulled into the driveway.

'You stay here,' she said.

Joseph saw me, and then he saw her getting out.

His arms at his sides.

Watching.

She went up to Joseph and stood close to him.

She reached out to touch him, but he moved back and away.

She let her arm go down and she said something.

He nodded.

She pointed back at the car, at me.

He shook his head.

She sighed.

She said something.

Joseph shook his head again.

Then the police showed up. They got out from their car, two guys. Two big guys. They walked up to the librarian and Joseph with that slow, big walk police have. They stood next to Joseph, and he backed up a little so they wouldn't be standing behind him. They talked to the librarian and she talked to them. She shook her head.

She said something to Joseph again.

He shook his head, and one of the big policemen put his arm on Joseph's.

Joseph pulled it away – which the big policeman did not like. He came closer. Joseph took a step back and I could tell what he was going to do – and where.

So, I guess, could the librarian.

She held out her hand and said something else. They all three looked at her. She said something else, and then she ran into the house.

Joseph watched her. He didn't even see the other policeman come around behind him, that's how hard he watched her.

Then she came out, kind of running, and in her hand was a photograph.

She gave it to Joseph and he looked at it. I could tell his hand was sort of trembling, but he never took his eyes off it. Then she put her arm behind Joseph's back – he was still looking at the photograph, so he didn't flinch – and she walked with him to her car. The big policemen watched, and she turned around and nodded to them. They let her go. And she brought Joseph to the back door of the car, opened it, and said, 'Get in.'

He looked up at her.

He looked behind him at the two policemen.

'Oh, Joseph, it's the best we can do for now. Please.'

I looked at the two policemen. They were still watching.

'Joseph,' I said.

He looked at me.

'What are you doing here?' he said.

'Looking for you,' I said.

He smiled. Really. He smiled. Number eight. Definitely not sort of.

He got in the car and leaned forwards. 'Look at this,' he said, and showed me Jupiter.

T HE librarian drove us back to Maine Street, where my parents were standing and looking around, waiting. When we got out and my mother saw Joseph, she ran towards him. He probably wasn't sure if she was going to hug him or slaughter him.

Probably she wasn't sure either.

She ended up hugging him. And my father did too.

Even Jupiter's foster mom hugged Joseph. 'You look so much alike,' she said. 'And determined, like she is.'

Joseph just listened. It was like he was dragging every word about Jupiter into himself so he could remember it and treasure it in his heart.

'We're taking good care of her,' she said.

'I'm her father,' said Joseph.

She looked at him. 'I'll tell her all about you,' she said. 'I'll write to you. I promise.'

And Joseph said, 'Tell her I . . .' He stopped. His mouth sort of crumpled.

'I will,' she said.

That was pretty much all Joseph said on the way home.

We stopped at a diner so he could get something to eat, since he hadn't eaten for most of two days except for the Baptist potato chips and breakfast with Pastor Greenleaf. I won't even tell you how much he ate, except my father had to look twice in his wallet to make sure he had enough money.

We got home in time for milking. Rosie did her happy moo when she saw Joseph.

Then at supper, he ate like we hadn't even stopped at the diner.

THAT night, Joseph stood by the window in the cold dark. He held Jupiter's picture, looked at it, looked up at the sky, looked back at the picture. I was almost asleep when he said, 'So, Jackie, you still have my back.'

'Yup. And it's Jack.'

'Yeah.' Then he looked up at Jupiter. 'Thanks,' he said.

I don't know if he ever went to bed that night.

Eight

OVER THE NEXT couple of days, Mrs Stroud had a lot to say to Joseph about violating rules and being mature and understanding boundaries, and what was he thinking anyway, and didn't he realize and stuff.

And over the next couple of days, Mr Canton had a lot to say to Joseph about missing school and about responsibilities and being truant and meeting expectations, and who did he think he was, and didn't he get it that rules are for everybody and stuff.

We started walking to school again, since Joseph really didn't want to hear the whole lot that Mr Haskell probably had to say too. My father said that was all right.

What Joseph did want to hear, though, was anything about Jupiter – and the librarian kept her promise: she wrote to Joseph every week. All through the rest of January and into February, the letters came – mostly on Mondays – and sometimes Joseph would read a little bit to us, or show the new picture, but mostly he kept them to himself, which my father said was all right too.

And you know what? At night now, I wasn't hearing anything from Stone Mountain.

It was still dark when we walked to school in the morning, but it was lighter coming home, and not as cold. Sometimes we'd have snowball fights by old First Congregational, and Joseph would defend from behind the Bridge Out sign, or sometimes we'd just lob snowballs at the bell. At home, sugaring time would come soon, and already we'd carried the pails and the taps and the tubing down from the barn loft and begun to wash them all out. Joseph and I were splitting wood – he was getting good – and piling it beside the sugaring house. And in the Small Barn, Quintus Sertorius had smelled February and already he was excited. He knew he'd be dragging the sled through the woods soon, and after a winter of doing not very much, he was ready to get out.

Things were changing for Joseph at school. He wasn't doing fifth-period Office Duty anymore, since Mr D'Ulney had nominated him for Math Olympiad in April, so fifth period he was tutoring Joseph in calculus.

No kidding. Calculus.

In PE, Coach Swieteck put Joseph in charge of his own squad of kids who wanted to go out for track and field in the spring. Joseph worked them in the field stuff – high jump and broad jump and even pole vault – and he was so good that no one minded that a kid was coaching them. Except I don't think Mr Canton liked it. Once he came to class and did a lot of pointing at Joseph, who was showing John Wall and Danny

Nations and his ear buds how to pile up the high-jump pads. But Coach Swieteck said something I think the class wasn't supposed to hear and Mr Canton left pretty quickly.

I wondered if Joseph *was* supposed to hear it, though.

And Mrs Halloway, in Language Arts, was calling on him a lot – I think because she saw Joseph reading *Walden*. She asked him if he liked it and he said he'd already read it once and he was reading it again, and she asked if he had read her favourite Thoreau book, *A Week on the Concord and Merrimack Rivers*, and he said, '*A Week on the* what?' and she took him to the library and they checked it out together.

You know how teachers are. If they get you to take out a book they love too, they're yours for life.

In the third week of February, on Monday, after Joseph finished reading the letter from the librarian that was waiting for him – and it was a good one, you could tell – we went out with my father and tapped thirty-six trees. 'These pails will fill pretty quick,' he said. 'I don't know what we ever did without you, Joseph.'

He just said it like that. Just like that. But after he said it, Joseph looked at him.

'Think we can put in another two dozen tomorrow?' my father said.

'Someday, Jupiter would love to do this,' said Joseph.

Now my father looked at him.

'Yes, she will,' he finally said.

'Really?' said Joseph.

'Let's go back up to the house,' said my father.

That night, my father and mother went into their room right after supper. They were in there for a long time. I think they might have made a phone call or two.

'Have I told you about the first time Maddie and I danced?' said Joseph.

'Yes,' I said.

'It was great,' he said.

'I know.'

'It really was,' he said, and then he looked down the

hall towards my parents' room, and went out to be with Rosie – smiling.

I'd lost count.

THE nights stayed cold, and the days warmed, and the sap flowed like it had never flowed before, and my father almost laughed at the number of pails we brought in, and brought in, and brought in every day. We could hardly wait to come home from school – Joseph said it was almost worth taking the school bus for, but not quite. So we half ran most of the way in the light that slanted against us, and it began to feel as if it had always been like this, like it would always be like this, until that day we came home and there was a new clean-white pickup by the barn, running with no one inside, and no one around, and Joseph slowed and stopped, and he looked at me, and he said, 'Jackie, go into the Big Barn.'

'Why?'

'Just do it, OK?'

He gave me his books, looked at the pickup again, and went inside.

I went into the barn, put our books down on the grain bins, and went to rub Rosie's rump – even though she'd rather have Joseph do it.

Waited.

Rubbed Dahlia's rump. She doesn't care who rubs her rump – she just keeps chewing.

Waited.

Went back out to the grain bins.

And then I heard my father holler, 'No!'

And then again, 'No!'

That was all I needed.

Here's what I saw when I slammed into the kitchen, less than one second later.

My mother standing behind Joseph, with her hands on his shoulders.

Joseph crying. His face all wet.

My father standing in front of the two of them.

Joseph's father standing by the door, so close I almost ran into his back.

And in his hand – I just saw it for a second – the blue metal of a gun.

Then Joseph's father had his arm around my chest, and he dragged me against him, and my father took a step towards us, and Joseph's father jerked me tight and said, 'Stop,' and my father did.

I could smell his father. The stink of sweat, the sick sweet of what he'd been drinking.

'This changes things,' he said.

No one spoke.

'This changes things,' he said again. He leaned towards my father. 'It sure does. All I want's my boy.' He shook me. 'Same as you.'

'We both want what's best for our boys,' said my father. I could tell he was trying to sound calm – but he wasn't. 'We both want what's best. But this isn't the way to do it.'

'It's my way,' said Joseph's father.

And then Joseph, from somewhere deep in his gut, screamed. 'You sold her! You freaking sold her!'

'I made an arrangement,' Joseph's father said. 'You weren't going to get her. And we needed a new truck. I'm not a do-good fool – like them.' He pointed to my parents.

Joseph screamed again. Not even words this time. He screamed at his father like something had ripped deep inside him.

Then, suddenly, he pulled away from my mother, and if my father hadn't grabbed him, he would have come at us.

My father held Joseph from behind, held him as he cried and sobbed, held him as he went to the floor.

And when Joseph sobbed into silence, his father said, 'Done now, kid?'

Joseph looked at him.

'Get in the truck.'

Joseph stood up. My father held his arm.

'In the truck,' his father said again.

My father pulled Joseph behind him.

'You're going to get in your truck,' my father said. 'You're going to let my boy go, and you're going to get in your truck, and this is going to end.'

But Joseph's father held me even tighter. 'You think you're in charge here?' he said. He held his hand out and showed the gun, then placed it against my side.

A cry jolted from my mother.

I think that was when I was about to wet my pants.

'Give me my boy and we'll be gone.'

My father said, 'And how far do you think you'll get? Ten miles? Fifteen? Maybe all the way to the state border, but they'll be watching for you there. Truck like yours, they'll find you easy.'

'So maybe I'll take both of them,' said Joseph's father. 'How'd you like that? I'll take my kid and yours for insurance.'

'No,' said Joseph. 'No. Dad, I'm coming. Let's go.'

He came out from behind my father.

'Let's go, Dad. Leave him here. Let's leave them all here and go.'

His father's arm around me relaxed a little.

Joseph came up to us slowly. 'Let's go,' he said, almost whispered.

I felt the gun move away from my side.

Joseph took my arm and pulled me away from his father. 'Dad, let's go.' He put his hand on my back and nudged me towards my father.

And Joseph, Joseph took his father's arm – 'C'mon' – and they went through the door, and outside. 'Let's go.'

The door closed.

My father ran to the phone, my mother to me.

I watched through the window as Joseph and his father got in the pickup. The door slammed and the pickup whipped around and away. Not before Joseph looked back one more time, and he saw me, and then he was gone.

They weren't ten seconds out of the yard before my father had the police on the phone.

• • •

HERE'S what we figured happened next.

Joseph's father was probably driving a whole lot faster than he could handle.

Mr Canton was driving out of school and he was about to turn right by old First Congregational when he saw the white pickup coming towards him.

He braked, and skidded on the ice into the middle of the road.

Joseph's father hit him square. He jammed Mr Canton's car over the embankment and into some trees – which kept it from rolling completely.

Then he turned in front of old First Congregational.

Through the Bridge Out sign.

Onto the Alliance bridge.

They didn't even make it halfway.

The rotted timbers collapsed and the pickup fell between the girders and then it went through the ice and was gone.

By the time Mr Canton got out of his car and ran

to the bridge, he couldn't see a thing in the black water.

Neither could the police later.

No one could see a thing.

T HEY didn't get the pickup out of the river for two days.

My father wouldn't let me go – but he went.

He said Mr Canton opened the frozen door on Joseph's side.

But it was my father who carried Joseph out of the truck.

That's all he would tell me.

T HE funeral service for Joseph was three days later.

Mr D'Ulney was there. Mr Canton. Mrs Halloway. Coach Swieteck, who cried the whole time.

My mother and father.

The librarian, who sat at the back.

Pastor Greenleaf from the Baptist church outside Lewiston.

Mrs Stroud.

Ernie Hupfer, John Wall, Danny Nations. No ear buds.

That was all.

We met in a side chapel of new First Congregational, because there were so few of us. We didn't sing, but Mrs Ballou played the organ quietly through about everything. Reverend Ballou asked if anyone had anything they'd like to say, and my father looked at me. But I didn't want to say anything in front of people. I might . . . you know.

So Reverend Ballou read some verses and talked about them and he said something about angels and he stopped for a little bit and then he said, really quiet, 'Where the hell were they?' and then we prayed a long time. Afterwards we went out to the cemetery on Lower Gore, where the Hurd grandparents and great-grandparents and great-great-grandparents are buried.

Mr Canton and Mr D'Ulney, and my father and I, we held the ropes that lowered Joseph into our family, beside the high white pines. Then Reverend Ballou prayed again, and he said that Joseph had put himself in danger to save others, and then he said, 'Greater love hath no man than this, that a man lay down his life for his friends.'

And that's when I started crying. Crying like a kindergarten kid in front of everyone. Crying because Joseph wasn't just my friend.

I had his back.

And he had mine.

That's what greater love is.

Nine

WE WAITED MORE than a year, and then, on what would have been Joseph's sixteenth birthday, when the apple trees were blooming and the bees doing their dances, Mrs Stroud drove into our yard.

In the back seat was Jupiter.

As soon as the door was opened and Mrs Stroud got her unstrapped, Jupiter was out and sort of waddling around, looking at everything, touching everything, smelling everything, as if she had a whole lot of time to make up for and she wasn't going to waste a second. Black eyes, black hair, a little less than middle for height, a little less than middle for weight, sort of middle for everything else.

She was smiling.

'Here she is,' said Mrs Stroud.

Jupiter stared at my parents – her parents too, now.

My father knelt down, and Jupiter put out her hand and pulled his nose, and laughed. Then my mother knelt down, and Jupiter put out her hand and stroked her cheek.

'Jupiter, this is your new brother,' said Mrs Stroud. 'His name is Jack.'

I knelt down, and Jupiter put out both her hands and pulled my ears.

'Jackie,' said Jupiter.

'That's right,' I said. 'Jackie.'

'Jackie,' Jupiter said again.

I stood and I took her hand and we waddled together, around the car, then around the yard. We went into the

Big Barn and I showed her the cows – she was a little afraid, but she'd be OK – and then out to the Near Field where Quintus Sertorius was grazing and looking like he didn't want to do anything else, but he perked his velvet ears when he heard Jupiter squeal. Then we came out to the yard again and Jupiter smiled and laughed and she waddled around my parents. And then she stopped, and she held up her hands, and she said 'Jackie.'

I knelt down and Jupiter got on my back. She closed her little arms around my neck. I stood and hefted her up.

She laid her head against me.

'Jackie.' She yawned. 'Jackie.'

'Jupiter,' I whispered back. 'Jupiter. I promise I'll always know where you are.'

'Jackie,' she said again.

And I carried her into the house.

When You Reach Me

REBECCA STEAD

Miranda's life is starting to unravel. Her best friend, Sal, gets punched by a kid on the street for what seems like no reason, and he shuts Miranda out of his life. Then the key Miranda's mum keeps hidden for emergencies is stolen, and a mysterious note arrives:

'I am coming to save your friend's life, and my own. I ask two favours. First, you must write me a letter.'

The notes keep coming, and whoever is leaving them knows things no one should know. Each message brings her closer to believing that only she can prevent a tragic death. Until the final note makes her think she's too late.

Winner of the John Newbery Medal 2010

Shortlisted for the Waterstone's Children's Book Prize

'Smart and mesmerising'
New York Times

9781849392129 £6.99

THE DOGS

ALLAN STRATTON

Cameron and his mom have been on the run for five years. His father is hunting them. At least, that's what Cameron's been told. When they settle in an isolated farmhouse, Cameron starts to see and hear things that aren't possible. Soon he's questioning everything he thought he knew – and his own mind.

Something is waiting for him, something from long ago. Cameron must uncover its dark secrets before it tears him apart.

'Brilliant, page-turning and eerie. Had me guessing to the very end'
Joseph Delaney

'Creepy, satisfying and exciting'
Bookseller

9781783442256 £7.99